HALTON CITY PUBLIC LIBRARY

3 1751 05000511 6

LP MYS PAT
Pattinson, James, 1915-
The honeymoon caper /

D1600380

HALTOM CITY PUBLIC LIBRARY

3201 Friendly Lane

Haltom City, TX 76117

(817) 222-7785

DEMCO

SPECIAL MESSAGE TO READERS

This book is published under the auspices of

THE ULVERSCROFT FOUNDATION

(registered charity No. 264873 UK)

Established in 1972 to provide funds for research, diagnosis and treatment of eye diseases. Examples of contributions made are: —

A new Children's Assessment Unit at Moorfield's Hospital, London.

•

Twin operating theatres at the Western Ophthalmic Hospital, London.

•

A Chair of Ophthalmology at the University of Leicester.

•

The establishment of a Royal Australian College of Ophthalmologists "Fellowship".

You can help further the work of the Foundation by making a donation or leaving a legacy. Every contribution, no matter how small, is received with gratitude. Please write for details to:

**THE ULVERSCROFT FOUNDATION,
The Green, Bradgate Road, Anstey,
Leicester LE7 7FU, England.
Telephone: (0116) 236 4325**

**In Australia write to:
THE ULVERSCROFT FOUNDATION,
c/o The Royal Australian College of
Ophthalmologists,
27, Commonwealth Street, Sydney,
N.S.W. 2010.**

THE HONEYMOON CAPER

Steve Brady was not happy about taking on the job of accompanying lovely Linda Manning to Finland — he had been involved with her on a previous occasion and had only narrowly escaped with his life. However, the money was a pretty big consideration so he agreed to go along. But a lot of little problems kept cropping up — like how to dispose of a dead body in the U.S.S.R., and how to get back across the Russo-Finnish border when you were badly wanted by the KGB!

Books by James Pattinson
in the Linford Mystery Library:

WILD JUSTICE
THE TELEPHONE MURDERS
AWAY WITH MURDER
THE ANTWERP APPOINTMENT

HALTOM CITY PUBLIC LIBRARY
JAMES PATTINSON

THE HONEYMOON CAPER

Complete and Unabridged

LINFORD
Leicester

First published in Great Britain in 1976 by
Robert Hale Limited
London

First Linford Edition
published 1998
by arrangement with
Robert Hale Limited
London

Copyright © 1976 by James Pattinson
All rights reserved

British Library CIP Data

Pattinson, James
    The honeymoon caper.—Large print ed.—
Linford mystery library
1. Detective and mystery stories
2. Large type books
I. Title
823.9′14 [F]

ISBN 0–7089–5345–X

Published by
F. A. Thorpe (Publishing) Ltd.
Anstey, Leicestershire

Set by Words & Graphics Ltd.
Anstey, Leicestershire
Printed and bound in Great Britain by
T. J. International Ltd., Padstow, Cornwall

This book is printed on acid-free paper

1

Proposition

It was six o'clock in the evening and Brady had just returned to the two rooms up two flights of stairs not far from Holloway Gaol which he called his flat when the visitors arrived. He had not been expecting any callers and he was not at all sure he wanted any. When he saw the girl he was still not sure.

Not that she was not the kind of girl any unattached male of his age might have been only too happy to see standing on his doorstep. Indeed, with all that gleaming dark hair and those eyes and that nose, with that mouth and that figure and a lot of other physical attributes too numerous to mention, she might well have been some kind of wish fulfilment. But not Brady's.

For the fact of the matter was that this was not the first time she had called on him. And that previous occasion — two years ago, was it? — had been the prelude to trouble, rather nasty trouble, for Stephen Brady. To be perfectly honest, of course, it had not been her fault — not all of it anyway — but he had an idea that trouble might come to him again if he had too much to do with her; it could be something that followed her around like a shadow, something to do with the kind of business she was in.

'Well,' he said; and his tone, if not exactly cool, was certainly not of the superheated variety either; it was strictly neutral because of that memory of what had happened before and the feeling that something of the same kind might conceivably happen again if he gave it half a chance. 'Well now, if it isn't Miss Manning as ever was. Or do I still call you Linda? It's been a long time.'

'Yes,' she said, 'it has, hasn't it? A year at least. But aren't you going to ask us to come in?'

And then he saw that this time she was not alone; hovering in the background was a sleek-looking character

2

who obviously knew where to go for the best clothes and was sufficiently well-heeled to be able to buy them without starving himself in the process. He was way above Brady in that respect; for the unpleasant fact was that Brady was feeling the pinch. Indeed, he was feeling it so much that it was beginning to hurt. Not that this was anything new: he seemed to spend a good deal of his time feeling pinches of one sort or another.

Still, that was no reason for keeping visitors standing outside on the landing, so he opened the door a bit wider and said: 'Well, of course. Do step inside.'

They came in, and Brady closed the door and Linda Manning made the introduction.

'This is Stewart Cobb.'

On a second inspection Cobb seemed even sleeker than he had the first time round; in fact he was just about the sleekest character Brady had ever seen: he had dark brown hair, a pale smooth face and a longish chin, and he looked as if he might have been around for maybe forty years or so; which would give him ten years more experience of all the nasty things in life than Brady had — if he ever encountered any of the nasty things. He was not quite as tall as Brady — five-ten perhaps, and slim: those expensive tailors probably loved working for him because he made their stuff look so good — quite apart from the profit motive. He held out a hand, and that was sleek too; Brady hardly liked to shake it because he felt as though he might be contaminating it with his own coarse touch, but he did so all the same.

'My name's Steve Brady. The lady forgot to mention it.'

'Yes, I know,' Cobb said; and he rescued his hand, and for a moment Brady thought he was going to wipe it on the handkerchief that was just visible in his breast-pocket; but he must have come to the conclusion that such an action might have been construed as rather insulting, or possibly he was reluctant to disturb the handkerchief, which looked as though it had been fitted by the people who made the suit, for he just gave it a brief inspection, winced ever so slightly and let it fall to his side.

'I suppose you would,' Brady said. It was something that Linda would hardly have omitted to tell him before bringing him along; though why she had brought him anyway was beyond Brady's powers of guessing; there ought to have been more profitable ways of spending a summer evening. If it came to that, why was she going around with someone like this Stewart Cobb at all? He was certainly not in her age group, as the statisticians might have said. But perhaps she liked sleek men older than herself; and when that thought crept into his mind he felt a stab of something that might almost have been jealousy, even though it was more than a year since he had stopped having any romantic ideas as far as Miss Manning was concerned.

There were two armchairs in the room, the kind people used to have delivered in plain vans before hire-purchase became so respectable you had to be eccentric to pay cash for anything except postage stamps. They were upholstered in some material called uncut moquette, which was pretty hard-wearing but not hard enough to resist getting worn through on the arms and one or two other places in the course of nearly forty years of tough use. Brady remembered his manners and invited his visitors to sit down, and Cobb seemed to have grave doubts about letting his suit come into contact with the uncut moquette, but he decided to take the plunge and maybe let the dry cleaners have a go at it afterwards.

'We wondered if you'd be in,' Linda said.

Brady sat on a tall stool that had once stood up against the bar in a pub and tried to think why he had ever lost touch with a girl as attractive as this. But it was not difficult to remember why: she had had other interests, and after one experience of getting mixed up in that kind of interest he had had enough and had decided that a quiet life was more in his line.

Seeing her again now, however, he began to wonder whether he had done the right thing. And then he remembered that he had really had no choice in the matter, because in fact it was she who had done the breaking off. So when you came to think about it she had a nerve to turn up again trailing this Stewart Cobb behind her as if to taunt him.

'I haven't been getting out much in the evenings lately,' Brady said. It was cheaper to stay in and read a library book, but he saw no reason why he should explain that to her. Or to Cobb either. Maybe least of all to Cobb. And then he said: 'You've had your hair done differently.'

'Yes,' she said, 'I have.'

'I like it,' Brady said. He had no idea what style you would have called it, but it was longer than it had been, though not so long that she had to keep hooking it out of her eyes; and it was still as black as a raven's wing, so she had obviously not taken to dyeing it. She was wearing a pale blue cotton dress which looked like a sports shirt at the top and had a zip up the front and a belt with a big white plastic buckle. Her shoes were the same colour as the dress and so was her handbag. He wondered whether the handbag had a gun in it this time, but he decided not to ask.

'Well,' she said, 'I'm glad you like it this way, Steve, because it would have been a pity if you hadn't.'

He failed to see just why his opinion concerning her hair style should have bothered her one way or the other, but maybe she simply liked to be admired. Most people did, and women especially.

'What are you doing these days?' she asked. 'Have you gone back to the antique business?'

He felt sure she knew damned well what he was doing these days, just as she had known that other time. She would have made inquiries and would have come up with the answer that he was doing very little; that he was out of a job and in the red. Perhaps that was why she was sitting in one of his armchairs right now. Perhaps there was some scheme in which he figured churning around in her lovely head. Well, he would hear all about it in due course, and when he did he might not be terribly eager to be involved.

'No,' he said, 'I haven't gone back to the antique business, so if you're looking for any more Victorian portable writing-desks, or maybe a set of Regency dining chairs, or even a flower-decorated chamber-pot, I'm afraid you'll have to search elsewhere.'

She shook her head, and the black hair executed a kind of swaying dance before settling back into its original position. 'I'm not looking for anything in the antique line.'

'Something rather less aged,' Cobb said, and he permitted himself a faint smile.

Brady was not much taken with the smile; if he had been asked to describe it in one word he would have called it cynical. And he had the impression that Cobb was looking at him in a slightly cynical way too. But there was also speculation in his eyes, and a horse-dealer sizing up the capabilities of an animal might have worn just such an expression as there was on his face at that moment. Brady was not sure that he liked being sized up — especially by a man like Cobb.

He turned to the girl. 'So if it's not antiques you've come for, what is it? Or are you going to tell me this is purely a social call — for old times' sake?'

'No, Steve, not purely social — though it is nice to see you again.'

'And if I'd known you were coming I'd have baked a cake,' Brady said. 'I'd offer you a drink if I had anything in the cellar, but at the moment stocks seem to have run out. If you'd care for a cup of tea, I can manage that.'

Cobb glanced at the battered gas-cooker and the sink half full of unwashed crockery and appeared to suppress a shudder.

'Not for me,' he said hurriedly.

'Linda? You know I make a good cup of char.'

'Yes, I know you do,' she said; and Cobb gave her an odd look, with eyebrows lifting ever so slightly, as though he could not imagine how she could ever have brought herself to drink tea in such squalid surroundings. 'But at the moment I'm not really thirsty. So let's just stick to business, shall we?'

'Well, certainly let's do that,' Brady said. 'If there is any business to stick to.'

She gave him a long steady look, and she had to tilt her head back a little to do it because, perched on the high stool, he rather overshadowed her. 'How does the idea of being my husband strike you?' she asked.

He nearly fell off the stool with shock. 'Your husband!'

'That's right.'

He wondered whether she were pulling his leg, but she was not laughing; she looked dead serious about it, and he had to be dead serious too.

'Are you making a proposal?'

'Not so much a proposal. More a proposition.'

'Perhaps you'd better explain that. I don't seem to be quite with you.'

'But I hope you will be. That's the idea, you see.'

'No, I'm sorry, but I don't see.'

'Well, it's like this — I have to go

on a journey and I need a husband to keep me company and sort of lend me respectability, if you understand.'

'I'm beginning to. Would this journey, by any possible chance, be to foreign parts?'

'Actually, yes.'

'I thought so. And it's to be a kind of honeymoon caper. Is that it?'

'Well,' she said, 'I suppose that would be one way of putting it.' But she sounded a shade doubtful all the same, as though the expression had conjured up the possibility of certain complications not in the original specification.

'And what would be the other way?'

Cobb put a word in then. 'It's not really for amusement,' he said. 'You must realise that.'

'Somehow,' Brady said, 'I didn't think it would be.' He looked at Linda, which was more pleasant than looking at Cobb. 'Do I really get round to marrying you or is it just window-dressing?'

'Just window-dressing.'

'I was afraid it might be. Now don't tell me you want me as a bodyguard. The way you handle a gun, why would you need any protection? And besides, you know that isn't my line. I'm a coward, remember?'

'Now, Steve,' she said, 'why must you always play yourself down? You're not really cowardly. Well, not much. And anyway, I'm not looking for a bodyguard, so don't let that worry you.'

'I'm relieved to hear it. At least, I would be if I really believed you. I mean, there's going to be trouble, isn't there?'

'Why should you think that?'

'It comes with the job, doesn't it?'

'Not necessarily. In fact, I don't think there'll be any trouble at all.'

Brady got off the stool and went to the sink and started filling the kettle; and then he remembered that nobody was in the market for any tea, and he turned the tap off and put the kettle down again.

'I'm sorry,' he said, 'but I just don't like the sound of it. My nerves took a nasty beating that time in Holland and I don't think they can absorb any more punishment in whatever country you intend travelling to.'

'It won't be like that this time.'

'Maybe it won't, but I'd rather not take the risk. So, if it's all the same to you, no thanks, Linda.'

'You'd be paid,' Cobb said; and he started to rub the arm of the chair with the tips of his fingers, realised suddenly what he was doing, and stopped in horror.

'How much?' Brady asked.

'Should we say two hundred pounds?'

'For that money there has to be trouble.'

Two hundred pounds was not such a lot with all the inflation there was knocking around, but it was a hell of a lot more than you would expect just for taking a holiday in company with an attractive girl. Some people would expect you to pay them for that kind of privilege; and a lot of people would be quite prepared to pay for it too. So the conclusion was that it was not going to be quite as nice and cosy as they were trying to make him believe. He never had believed it anyway.

'There doesn't have to be trouble,'

Cobb said. 'Of course there may be some slight danger.' He made it sound utterly negligible and hardly worth mentioning. 'But where could you say for certain that there was no danger? In your own bed you might be blown up by a gas explosion. And cars! Do you know that a thousand people a week are killed on the highways of the United States? That they've already topped the two million mark for road slaughter?'

'So it's America I'm supposed to go to for my two hundred quid?'

'No, it isn't America.' Cobb seemed in danger of losing his patience. 'Look, if you don't want the job I'm sure we can easily find someone else who does.'

'So why did you come to me?'

'It was Miss Manning's idea. She seems to think she can trust you.'

'Oh?' Brady looked at her. 'Is that so?'

She gave him a lovely smile. 'There's nobody I'd rather trust. Nobody.'

Brady was flattered. He tried not to be, but he was. And he began to think that, while two hundred pounds was certainly no fortune, equally certainly it was something he could find a very good use for just then. And maybe after all there would not be any trouble; or at least not too much. So what the hell! Why not give it a run?

'I think the fee is a bit low,' he said; and he knew by the way those wonderful dark eyes that Linda Manning carried around with her suddenly lighted up that she knew she had him hooked.

'It's the most we can manage,' Cobb said. 'You mustn't run away with the idea that we're made of money. As a matter of fact there's a bit of an economy drive on just now and things are really very tight.' He sounded like a confounded accountant, Brady thought, keeping an eagle eye on the petty cash. 'And all things considered, two hundred pounds is not at all a bad fee, not at all bad. It shouldn't take more than two or three weeks at the most, and of course all expenses will be taken care of.'

'Does that include the bridegroom's outfit? My wardrobe seems to be a bit depleted, and I'm sure you wouldn't want me to disgrace my wife by dressing like a tramp.'

Cobb frowned. 'We could perhaps give you a small advance — on account.'

'That isn't quite what I had in mind. Something more in the way of extra expenses, if you get me.'

'I think that's reasonable,' Linda said.

Cobb looked at her sourly. 'These things have to be approved. It's not as easy as you seem to think.'

'Don't be silly,' she said. 'It won't break the bank to give a hand-out for a new suit and a pair of shoes and some shirts and things.'

'You don't understand,' Cobb said; and Brady could see that he was not at all pleased by the suggestion that he was being silly. 'There are certain formalities to be observed in matters of this description. I can't just hand out expenses like that.'

'If you don't, the deal's off,' Brady said. With Linda backing him he felt he was on firm ground.

Cobb began to waver. 'It's highly irregular, it really is. How much do you need to fit yourself up?'

'I couldn't do it on less than fifty. You know what things cost these days. Even that would be skimping.'

'Fifty pounds!' Cobb looked shocked.

'The suit you're wearing cost a lot more than that.'

'Yes — well, that's quite a different matter.'

'Oh, why don't you stop haggling and give him the money?' Linda said. 'You know you can screw it out of the expense account.'

'That's all very well,' Cobb said; but he took a notecase from his pocket and extracted five ten-pound notes and handed them to Brady. It seemed to hurt him, but he did it.

'Thanks,' Brady said. 'Do you want a receipt?'

'That won't be necessary.'

Linda Manning watched Brady fold the notes and slip them into his hip-pocket. 'So you've decided to take the job, Steve?'

Brady sighed. 'It looks like it. And now maybe you wouldn't mind telling me where we're proposing to spend our honeymoon.'

'But of course I don't mind,' she said. 'It's Finland.'

'Oh,' Brady said; and it came into his head that Finland was awfully close to Soviet Russia. He was not sure whether or not there was any significance in that, but he was afraid there might be, and he had a queasy feeling in the stomach, as though he had eaten something which had not agreed with him — like a dose of arsenic maybe. 'Finland.'

He looked at Stewart Cobb, and Cobb gave him a wintry smile and nodded ever so slightly, while his eyes gave the impression of having been made from polished steel.

'Finland.'

2

In Touch

It was perhaps fortunate, Brady reflected, that the trip to Finland was taking place in the summer and not the winter: men's wear seemed to have shot up even further in price since he had last been around the outfitters, and fifty pounds would certainly not have gone far in the fur hat and sheepskin coat stakes, even without such accessories as skis and snow-shoes. He thought of trying to open a credit account, but decided it was not on: stores might advertise practically unlimited credit terms, but when it came to the bite they usually wanted bank references and suchlike proofs of an eventual ability to liquidate any debts that might be incurred. All he could have offered in that respect was a promise of two hundred pounds from some unspecified government department on the completion of a certain mysterious assignment in Finland, and he doubted whether any men's outfitter in his right mind would accept that kind of security. Quite apart from the fact that it was probably an official secret anyway.

For a week after the visit of Stewart Cobb and Linda Manning he saw nothing more of either of them. They would, Cobb had said, let him know when a date for departure had been fixed.

'There are certain arrangements to be made, but you'll get plenty of warning.'

'I don't need much warning,' Brady told him. 'I've got no commitments and I'm not going anywhere.'

'You're going to Finland,' Linda said.

'Yes, of course — on the honeymoon caper. I meant apart from that.'

Cobb had taken his passport. 'It needs a Finnish visa.'

'Is that necessary just for a visit?' Brady asked. 'I thought the Finns were pretty easy-going.'

'Best be on the safe side.'

'I'm certainly with you there,' Brady said. 'But shouldn't I get the visa?'

Cobb had given his wintry smile. 'I think it would be best if we saw to it.'

Brady had handed over the passport, and after that Cobb had said that as there was really nothing more to discuss they would be on their way.

'You're sure you won't change your mind about the tea?'

Cobb had taken another look at the choked-up sink, had winced again, and had shaken his head. 'Some other time perhaps.'

Brady had seen them to the top of the stairs but had not gone down to the door. He had noticed that Cobb avoided resting his hand on the banister rail.

'I'll be in touch,' Linda had said, and then they had gone.

It was now seven days later and she had not yet been in touch. He might have got in touch with her if he had known where she was living, but she had always been rather secretive on that point. And he could not make contact through the government department for which she worked because he had no idea which department it was. It was all so hush-hush anyway that he would probably never have got through the red tape entanglements.

The same went for Stewart Cobb. Cobb had gone off with his passport, and if he decided not to return it, it was probably gone for good. But there was no reason why he should not return it; there was a job to be done and Cobb had certainly not been fooling about that, otherwise he would never have forked out fifty quid. He would be back. Unfortunately.

But it was not Cobb who came, it was Linda. Which suited Brady: he had not really taken to Cobb and was not terribly keen on seeing him again, though he supposed he was bound to do so eventually.

It was one of those sultry evenings with a threat of thunder in the air. Brady had been out to get a snack at the pub round the corner, and when he returned he met her coming down the stairs and looking annoyed.

'Where have you been?' she demanded.

'Out,' Brady said.

'I've been knocking on your door and getting no reply.'

'You weren't likely to. Nobody to give one. I don't sit in there all the time, you know; sometimes I venture out into the world. I'm sorry if I've kept you waiting.'

'It doesn't matter,' she said in a slightly more conciliatory tone. 'After all, you didn't know I would be calling this evening, did you?'

'You didn't give me a firm date.'

'Well, let's not stand here on the stairs.' She turned and went up ahead of him and waited for him to unlock the door.

He let her go in first, then followed and closed the door. He noticed that she was wearing a different outfit and that she was carrying an umbrella as well as the handbag, so he guessed she had been listening to the weather forecast or taking a feel of her seaweed.

'You're expecting rain?'

'Let's not discuss the weather,' she said. 'I've brought your passport.'

She dipped in her handbag, fished it

24

out and handed it to him. He flipped through it and saw that something had been added which Cobb had not seen fit to mention; something, moreover, which he was none too happy about.

'I thought this was to be a trip to Finland,' he said.

'So it is.'

'Then why the Russian visa?'

She sat down in the armchair which Cobb had occupied during the previous visit. She appeared less worried about the uncut moquette than he had been.

'It would be pretty silly to go up there without one, wouldn't it? Think of the bother it could cause.'

'Why should it cause any bother?'

'Suppose we wanted to pop across the border.'

'I have no desire at all to pop across the border. Nothing has ever been further from my mind.'

'I'm surprised at you, Steve,' she said; and she really did look a little disappointed with him. 'Haven't you ever felt the urge to take a close look at Mother Russia?'

'That kind of urge has never been so strong that it's taken any great effort of self-denial to resist it. And frankly, Linda, if I did think of going there I wouldn't choose you for a travelling companion.'

The corners of her mouth went down slightly. 'Now really, Steve darling, that's not at all a nice thing to say.'

'Oh, it's nothing personal,' he hurried to assure her. 'You're very lovely, and all other things being equal, there's no one I'd rather have around the place. In fact, I might even find it possible to fall in love with you. Given the time.'

She opened her eyes very wide and stared at him. 'Would that be altogether wise?'

'No, it wouldn't be wise. It would be absolutely crazy. Because you're trouble, aren't you, Linda? You were trouble in Holland and I have a nasty feeling you could be trouble in Finland. But in Russia I haven't the slightest shadow of a doubt that you'd be trouble with a capital tee.'

She made no comment on that. All she

said was: 'Speaking of tea, I wouldn't refuse this time if you offered me a cup.'

He knew that she was sliding away from the Russian question, but there was nothing much he could do about it. He was committed now; and having already got rid of most of Stewart Cobb's fifty pounds, he could hardly withdraw because of an extra visa in his passport. He moved to the sink and filled the kettle and took the old brown teapot from the shelf above the cooker.

She was rummaging in her handbag again. 'You'd better have this too,' she said.

'What is it?'

'Your International Driving Permit.'

'So I'm to do some driving?'

'Well, you never know. We might hire a car. The Finnish scenery is lovely.'

'You've been there before?'

'No, but I've been told about it.'

He wondered whether she was telling the truth; he could never be certain with her. Not that she was given to telling lies in the ordinary way, but where her work was concerned it was a different matter; she would probably not have regarded it as lying at all — just prevarication in the line of duty.

He took the permit and then spooned some tea into the pot from the old biscuit-tin he used as a caddy. He took a bottle of milk from the refrigerator and a pair of cups from the hooks, and when the kettle boiled he made the tea. And all the time he was thinking he must have taken leave of his senses to let Cobb and Linda talk him into taking a job like this when all he really wanted was a quiet life and no excitement; at least, not the kind of excitement which this might lead to.

'By the way,' he said, 'I suppose that Russian visa is on the level?'

'What do you mean on the level?' she asked.

'I mean is it genuine?'

'Don't you think it looks genuine?'

'I wouldn't know. I've never seen one before.'

'So what makes you think it isn't?'

'Nothing. It's just this odd feeling I have that everything is a bit phoney.'

'You shouldn't have feelings like that.'

He noticed that she had avoided giving him a straight answer to the question. He poured the tea and handed her a cup.

'I suppose you've got a passport too?'

'Naturally.'

'In the name of Mrs. Brady?'

'Yes.'

'Well, that's certainly not genuine. Suppose somebody wants to see the marriage certificate.'

'I see no reason why anybody should.' She put the cup down and dipped again into her handbag. 'But if they do, there's no need to worry.' She pulled out a folded sheet of paper. 'Read it.'

Brady read it. It was all there, every relevant detail, including the registrar's signature. He refolded it and handed it back to her.

'What a pity we couldn't have had a church wedding. You'd have looked nice in a veil.'

She put the certificate back in her handbag. 'You'd have had to hire a morning suit. Think of the expense.'

'That's true,' Brady said. And then:

'Who exactly is Cobb? Is he the one who gives you your orders?'

She took a sip of tea before answering, and then all she said was: 'You ask too many questions. It's a bad habit.'

'And you don't intend to answer them?'

'No.'

'So I'm to be left in the dark?'

'It's the best way.'

'It may seem so to you, but I don't like travelling blind. It gives me an uneasy feeling.'

'Well,' she said, 'I'm sorry about that, Steve darling, but that's the way it's going to be.'

She finished her tea and stood up.

'You're not leaving already?' Brady said.

She gave him a cool look. 'Were you expecting me to stay?'

'Why not? Seeing that we're married and have a piece of paper to prove it.'

'Don't let that marriage certificate fool you.' She glanced round the room, and for a moment he had the impression that she had been taking lessons from Stewart

Cobb in the art of disdain. 'It's not much of a bridal suite, is it?'

'We could go to your place if that would suit you any better.'

'It wouldn't suit me at all. And I do hope you're not getting any silly ideas into your head. You've got to remember that all this is strictly a business deal.'

'I'm going to find that a bit difficult with you around all the time.'

She moved to the door.

'Would you like me to get you a taxi?' Brady asked. 'Or have you got a car?'

'I haven't got a car, but don't bother about the taxi; it's not far to the tube station.'

'Well, if that's the way you're travelling I'll walk you there. Unless you're going to object to that too.'

'No,' she said, 'I see no reason to object to that.' And she gave him a smile. Which was something.

As she had said, it was not far: about fifty yards to the Caledonian Road, another three hundred yards or so at a leisurely stroll, and they were there.

'It's the Piccadilly line,' Brady said.

31

'But I suppose you know that.'

'Yes, I know. Thanks for the company.'

'I may as well finish the job and see you on to the train.'

'There's no need.'

'I know, but I'd like to.'

She shrugged. 'All right then.'

They waited on the platform, and there was that tube smell and the posters advertising whisky and insurance and stretch bras, the electric rail gleaming dully and the tunnel opening at each end like a monstrous rat-hole. There were a few other passengers waiting, looking bored, and then the drunk appeared.

At least Brady supposed he was drunk; he had the slouching drunk's walk, staggering a little, as if at any moment he might fall down, yet never quite doing so. He was tall and thin, and his face had a kind of ravaged look, the skin yellowy and pockmarked; you could imagine someone had been gouging bits out of it here and there with a small pick. His eyes were dull, unfocused. He was wearing a washed-out denim shirt and check trousers very wide at the bottom, and people were avoiding him, the way people do with drunks, thinking maybe he would clutch at them to hold himself up and not wanting to get involved. A couple of young girls were giggling.

There was a seat by the wall, and he made it to the seat and flopped down on it and held his head in his hands, his elbows resting on his knees. He was really in a bad way. Brady was thankful not to have that head.

'I'll bet it's all swimming around inside there.'

Linda glanced at him questioningly.

'His head. I'll bet he's feeling like death. He must have been knocking it back.'

And then it occurred to him that the man might not be drunk but drugged. In spite of that ravaged face he could have been young enough for the drug scene. But either way he was not feeling good, not good at all.

Brady lost interest in him. The train seemed to be a long time coming and more passengers had dribbled on to the platform. He looked at Linda and thought again what a pity it was that she had to be doing this kind of business, because one way and another it was a pretty sordid business, with a lot of bribery and corruption, and double-crossing and double-double-crossing, and now and then a bit of killing thrown in to make the weight, and surely to goodness she was far too nice a girl for that sort of thing. She had once told him she was in it because it ran in the family. He had never met the family, and if that was what ran in it he never wanted to; but she could have been kidding.

'Have you ever thought of retiring?' he asked.

The idea seemed to amuse her. 'Do I look that old?'

'You don't look that old or any old,' Brady said. 'And maybe you never will if you don't get out while the going's good.'

'And what would I do if I got out?'

'Well now,' he said, 'I could think of plenty of things. You might even marry me for real.'

'And what would we live on?'

'That's a good question,' Brady said.

He heard the train coming. The drunk — if he was a drunk — must have heard it too; he got himself up on to his feet and stood with one hand on the wall, teetering. Brady wondered whether he would fall flat on his face as soon as he launched himself away from the wall, and he had half a mind to offer the man a bit of help, but decided not to. If you went around giving aid to drunks, where did it end?

He was standing on Linda's right, about a yard from the edge of the platform when the train appeared in the tunnel opening. He had turned his back on the drunk, and that was a mistake; he should have watched him. It might have been instinct that made him glance over his shoulder, a premonition perhaps, though he was no believer in premonitions; so maybe it was just idle curiosity, a desire to see how the drunk was managing. And it was as well he did so, for the drunk was managing not at all badly, all things considered. In fact he had got to within a couple of paces of Brady and Linda, and he was moving fast. Brady saw his eyes, and there was nothing unfocused about them now; the man knew where he was going and what he was doing, and Brady knew too.

He grabbed Linda and dragged her aside, and it was only just in time; the drunk's shoulder brushed her as he went past. He seemed to make a last desperate effort to stop, but he was too close to the edge and had too much momentum. He fell on to the rails and the train hit him.

Some women screamed; the train came to a halt in the wrong place, still partly in the tunnel; a man fainted.

Brady became aware of Linda tugging at his sleeve. He looked at her.

'Quick,' she said, and there was urgency in her voice. 'Let's get out of this.'

'But — '

'Don't argue. Let's go.'

He allowed her to persuade him. Some officials were running up. The driver was getting out of his cab, looking sick. A woman seemed to be having hysterics.

The drunk lay on the track with his head under the train.

They got out of there fast.

They walked along the Caledonian Road, taking it more slowly. Thunder was still muttering around and the sky was leaden, but it had not started to rain.

'Why the hurry to get away?' Brady asked.

'Because we can't afford to get ourselves mixed up with a suicide case.'

'It wasn't suicide,' Brady said.

'An accident then.'

'Not an accident either.'

'Now what are you trying to tell me?' she asked.

'He wasn't drunk; it was just an act. He meant to kill you.'

She came to a halt and stared at him. 'You're imagining things. He was drunk; he could hardly hold himself up. You saw him.'

'Yes, I saw him,' Brady said. 'I saw him just before he fell off the platform. And I'm damned sure he was no more drunk than I am. He meant to hit you, I know he did.'

She began to walk on again. 'I don't believe it,' she said, but she did not sound so sure.

'Had you ever seen him before?'

She shook her head.

'Not following you?'

'No.'

'He could have been all the same. He could have tailed you to the flat and then tailed us back to the tube.'

'Did you see him doing that?'

'No, but I wasn't looking for a tail.'

'I still think you're imagining things,' she said. 'Why would he want to kill me?'

'He could have been hired to do it.'

'By whom?'

'By someone who didn't want you to go to Finland perhaps.'

She seemed a trifle thoughtful after that, and Brady guessed that she was thinking there might be something in what he had said. He was thinking about it too, not very happily, for if there were people prepared to murder her in order to prevent her from going to Finland they must have strong reasons for not wishing her to go there. And if she did eventually get there they might have another shot at doing what they had so narrowly failed to do in London. It might even become something of a habit; in which case the honeymoon caper was not going to be the most enjoyable of capers, to say the least of it.

'Don't you think we ought to call the whole thing off?'

She gave him a sharp glance and nearly bumped into a man who looked as if he would not have minded how many times she did that.

'Why?'

'Because I'm beginning to think it may not be particularly healthy in Finland.'

'That's nonsense,' she said. 'Everybody knows it's one of the most hygienic countries in the world.'

'You know that's not what I meant. No amount of hygiene is going to help you if you get shoved into a train.'

'Then we'll just have to keep away from trains, won't we?'

He realised that nothing he could say was going to put her off the Finland trip, and he supposed that nearly being killed by a sham drunk, or even a genuine junkie, was all part of the job and to be taken in her stride, so he resigned himself to earning his two hundred pounds the hard way — with a lot of frayed nerves.

He saw her on to a bus, which seemed a better idea than going back to the tube, and just before it whisked her away he asked her whether the date for departure had yet been fixed.

'Damn!' she said. 'I should have told you. It's Thursday. I'll be in touch.'

He had to run along beside the bus to catch the last bit of information, and when he stopped running he remembered that today was Tuesday and that there was not a lot of it left. So much for Cobb's promise to give him plenty of warning.

Not that it made any difference.

3

The Last Word

Brady found the flight from London to Helsinki tedious. But to his way of thinking all journeys by air were tedious; they served the purpose of getting you from one place to another in the least possible time, but they lacked the charm of a sea voyage or even a train ride. Still, it was the modern way, and until the supply of fuel oil became exhausted, which would be around the year 1995 according to the experts, he supposed it would continue to be the way. What happened when there was no more oil was anybody's guess; maybe all the airliners would be grounded and become museum pieces, the dinosaurs of the Twentieth Century.

Rather to his surprise, Cobb had turned up to see them off, looking as sleek as ever in a dark grey suit and a bowler hat, and carrying the kind of umbrella that was surely never meant to be unrolled. Brady thought he passed something to Linda Manning, but it was done so unobtrusively that he could not be absolutely certain. Cobb seized an opportunity to take Brady on one side and thank him for saving Linda from a sticky death under the wheels of a tube train.

'So she told you about it?'

'Yes. And I must say it was a smart piece of work on your part; an admirably quick reaction.'

'It was instinctive. There was no time to think.'

'Instinctive or not, there can be little doubt that you saved her life.'

'You think it was an attempt to kill her?'

'I wouldn't like to say. There is that possibility of course. But where would be the motive?'

'To prevent her going to Finland and carrying out whatever operation she's going there to carry out.'

'That would be to assume that certain

42

highly secret information had leaked out.'

'Is that an impossibility?'

'Not an impossibility, no.' Cobb was frowning slightly, as though an unwelcome thought had crossed his mind. 'But most unlikely, I think.'

'That may be what you think, or what you'd like to think, but if you want my opinion, we've been rumbled and you ought to call it off.'

'Call it off! But that's simply not possible now.' He made a curiously helpless gesture. 'I couldn't do that even if I wanted to. I haven't the authority.'

Brady gathered from this that Cobb himself had not initiated the operation but was merely a link in the chain of command.

'Am I to take it then that if you did have the authority you would scrub it?'

Cobb gave a wry smile. 'Now, Brady, you really mustn't start putting words into my mouth.'

Brady got the impression that the answer might well have been yes if Cobb had not been far too cagey to admit as much.

'Couldn't you use a bit of persuasion?'

'At this late hour? Quite out of the question.'

'So you're prepared to let Linda risk her life for the sake of some crazy plan?'

'It is not a crazy plan, and you have no right to put it like that.' Cobb sounded annoyed but also seemed faintly embarrassed. 'You don't understand these things, how they are arranged. You are — and please don't take offence at the term — an outsider.'

'Don't you think I'm an insider now?'

'Not really. You are — how shall I put it? — an auxiliary, on a purely temporary basis.'

'It could be very temporary indeed.'

'Now you're being pessimistic. You do, if I may say so, tend to take a far too gloomy view of things. There is no point in always expecting the worst to happen; it merely serves to induce a feeling of depression and lower the morale.'

Which was easy enough to say, Brady reflected; especially when you were not standing in the direct line of fire. He doubted whether Cobb would have any sleepless nights from worrying about possible dangers to a couple of pawns in Finland.

Yet he could have been wrong about that, for Cobb suddenly gripped his arm and said earnestly: 'Look after her, Brady.'

Brady, rather surprised by this show of feeling in such an apparently cold fish, said: 'I'll do what I can.'

Cobb released his arm. 'I'm sure you will. Yes, I'm sure you will.'

It crossed Brady's mind that Cobb, as Linda's immediate superior, perhaps took a kind of fatherly interest in her. And then he wondered whether fatherly was quite the right word. Or brotherly either if it came to the point. Somehow or other he found the thought faintly displeasing.

★ ★ ★

It was early afternoon when they got through the airport customs and squeezed themselves on to the bus that was to take them into Helsinki. The bus was crowded, and most of the people who were crowding it had the blue-eyed, fair-haired Scandinavian look. Brady and Linda were exceptions; conspicuous exceptions it seemed to Brady, and he would have felt safer if they could have blended more successfully with the northern background. All the way from London he had been looking for suspicious characters, but the trouble was that when you started looking for suspicious characters practically everyone in sight began to look suspicious, even the air hostesses, and it became an unprofitable occupation. He told himself to cut it out, because if he went on like that he was going to be a nervous wreck before they had been in Finland a couple of days. But five minutes later he was at it again.

After some delay the bus got going and he asked Linda a question he had not thought to ask until then.

'Do you speak Finnish?'

'No,' she said, 'but don't worry; we'll manage very well with English.'

'That's the typical British approach, isn't it? I'd have thought in your profession you'd have been a bit more thorough.'

'Never mind my profession.' She sounded a trifle sharp. 'Just remember we're here for a holiday. You might even try to look a little less depressed about it and have a shot at giving the impression that you're enjoying life.'

'I never was much of an impressionist.'

'Oh, for goodness' sake,' she said. 'I'm beginning to wish I hadn't brought you along.'

'Well, you can't say it was my idea.'

'Ha!' she said, and neither of them spoke another word until they were in Helsinki.

It was much as Brady had expected it to be — a lot of glass-and-granite buildings and wide streets laid out on the gridiron pattern. He remembered that it had not always been the capital; when the country had been under Swedish rule the capital had been Turku, but the Russians had switched it to Helsinki in 1812. He had come across that information in a guide-book, and also the fact that, except for Reykjavik, it was the most northerly European capital with a population of just over half a million. None of which provided any answer to the question that really mattered: what in hell did Linda propose doing there and why had it been considered necessary to drag him along for company?

They got a taxi on leaving the bus, and the taxi took them to one of those square blocks of granite and glass which turned out to be the hotel where there was a room reserved for them. Brady paid the driver with some of the Finnish marks which Linda had slipped to him during the flight, and they walked into the hotel and checked in at the desk and produced their passports and were shown to their room.

The room put him in mind of a London furniture store putting on a Scandinavian week: everything had that stark, clinical look, utterly lacking in any superfluous ornamentation, as though anything not strictly utilitarian were immoral or even indecent. He saw that there were twin beds, which was interesting if scarcely exciting, and there was a bathroom that had just about everything.

'What now?' he asked. It was still only half-past four, and at this time of the year it probably got dark somewhere around midnight — if then. Nobody in his senses would choose Finland in summer for a honeymoon.

'We could go for a walk,' she said. 'If you're not too tired.'

'Why should I be tired?'

'No reason. Do you want to go for a walk?'

'Well, it's a bit early for bed, isn't it? I suppose we may as well have a look at the city.'

'I'll take a shower first,' she said. 'Then we'll go.'

He sat on a chair and listened to the shower and reflected that they were certainly not in Finland just so that they could walk round Helsinki and wait for bedtime. But maybe nothing had been lined up for the first day.

★ ★ ★

Linda Manning seemed to have an inexhaustible supply of energy and an inexhaustible urge for sight-seeing. By the time they had looked at the Senate Square with its statue of Czar Alexander II, at the Great Church and the Russian Orthodox Trinity Church, the Government Palace and the University, after they had window-shopped along Alexander Street and had admired the design of the Railway Station with its 155 feet high granite tower, after they had gazed pop-eyed at a score of other buildings and monuments, Brady's feet were killing him and he felt as limp as a used handkerchief. Linda at last became aware of his steadily decreasing interest in architecture and statuary and suggested that he had perhaps had enough.

Brady admitted that he had. 'It gets a bit wearing after a time.'

'Frankly,' she said, 'I don't think you had much zest for it in the first place.'

'You could be right. I once spent a month in Aberdeen and I've never really had the taste for granite since then.'

'Perhaps we should go and eat.'

'Now that does seem a good idea.'

They ate at a restaurant called the Walhalla, which was a name to conjure up visions of Viking warriors wassailing through the night. But in fact there was nothing quite as exciting as that. The food was good if not exactly exciting either, and when they had finished Brady sat back feeling very nicely filled and letting his feet take a rest from the punishment. At the same time he studied Linda Manning, temporarily Mrs. Stephen Brady, and thought how much more pleasant that kind of exercise was than gazing at blocks of granite and the domes of churches.

'They held the Olympic Games here in 1952, you know,' she said.

'In here?' It was a big restaurant, but not that big.

'In Helsinki, idiot. The Olympic Village is now a suburb, I believe. We could have had a look at it if we'd had the time.'

'And we haven't?'

'We're leaving tomorrow,' she said.

It was the first he had heard about that.

'So it's to be a one-night stand. Where do we go next?'

'Porvoo.'

'Where's that?'

'Haven't you even taken the trouble to look at a map? It's further along the coast — about thirty miles east of here.'

'And what do we do there?'

She gave an enigmatic smile. 'Now, Steve darling,' she said, 'why don't you just wait and see?'

Thirty miles further east made it thirty miles nearer the Russian border. He would have felt happier if they had been going to Turku, because that was in the other direction; but she was the boss.

There were a lot of solid-looking citizens dining in the Walhalla, and he noticed one or two of the men glance at Linda; but that meant nothing, except that she was worth glancing at. There was no one he would have picked out on sight as a likely killer; but how did you identify a killer simply by looking at him? The seeming drunk at the tube station in London had given no impression of homicidal tendencies until the last moment; and then it had been almost too late. So any one of these solid, square-shouldered men placidly shovelling the calories on board might turn out to be the murderous kind with designs on the life of Mrs. Stephen Brady; and even on the life of Mr. Stephen Brady too if it came to that. Happy thought.

He paid for the meal with some more of the marks with which she had provided him. They were really only loaned to him so that he could look like the big spender, since it might have appeared strange if she had done the paying, and they were coming out of the expense account anyway, so it made no difference.

'And what now?'

'We could do some more sight-seeing,' Linda suggested. 'Unless you really are tired this time.'

'I really am tired this time,' Brady said.

In the end they went to a cinema. It seemed a hell of a thing to do — all the way to Helsinki to see a flick — but how else did you kill time and take the load off your feet? It was a Swedish film, and about as gloomy as Swedish films usually were. Even without being able to understand the dialogue you could tell it was gloomy by the way the characters were acting and by the agonised expressions on their faces. It did nothing to raise Brady's spirits.

'Why do the Swedes all have such tortured souls?'

'One theory is,' Linda said, 'that it's because they haven't had a war for more than a century. War has a therapeutic effect on people.'

'Like the Vietnam war had on the Americans?'

'You don't have to be difficult,' she said.

They went back to the hotel and got the key and went up in the lift to the room on the third floor, and he wondered whether to do one of those abrupt entrances that you saw in the TV thrillers, where the hero flings the door open and makes a dive for cover to avoid the bullets. And then it occurred to him that Mrs. Stephen Brady might be carrying a gun for self-protection, and he paused with the key in the lock and asked her if she was.

'Are you crazy?' she said. 'Do you think I want to get myself arrested?'

'You had a gun in Holland.'

'That was different,' she said, though she omitted to explain what the difference was. 'And when are you going to open that door?'

He decided to skip the theatricals and just open the door in the normal way, and if any bullets started flying around that would be just too bad. His heart raced a bit when he walked in, but there was no one waiting to take a shot at him or stick a knife in his ribs, and after he had looked in the bathroom and the wardrobe and under the beds the pulse settled down to something like its normal rate of working.

Linda watched him with a faintly amused expression, apparently not sharing his misgivings.

'What are you looking for?' she asked.

'I don't know,' Brady said, 'but whatever it is, I just hope I don't find it.'

She offered him the choice of beds, and when he suggested that they were pretty big for singles and it was hardly worth while rumpling both of them if they were leaving in the morning, she soon put a damper on that bright idea.

'Isn't it time you got it into your head that we're here simply to do a job of work? Please remember that you're only playing a part.'

'I was trying to get into the spirit of the character.'

'The character doesn't have to be as spirited as that. Do you want to use the bathroom first?'

'No; you can.'

He could hear her moving around in there and the sound of running water, and when she came back she was wearing pale blue pyjamas and looking lovely.

'It's all yours.'

'You mean you've changed your mind?' Brady asked.

'I was referring to the bathroom,' she said, and she sounded unamused.

He looked at her. 'You've forgotten to put your hair in curlers.'

She turned the covers back and got into bed without even bothering to answer that one. He watched her settling down, and her composure nettled him.

'Aren't you afraid I might rape you?'

She turned her head on the pillow and treated him to a long, cool look. 'Do you really think you're capable of that, Steve darling?' she asked.

He went to the bathroom feeling that somehow or other she had had the last word. When he came back she was already asleep, so he supposed she had.

4

Porvoo

They travelled by bus to Porvoo. The bus was almost as crowded as the one that had brought them from the airport and the road followed a curving route roughly parallel to the line of the coast. Brady was crushed between Linda and a stout middle-aged woman with a basket on her lap who turned to him now and then, made some remark which he could not understand and smiled broadly. Brady smiled back at her, which seemed to be all the answer she required, and whenever the bus gave a lurch he found himself thrown heavily against her ample bosom, which he found far more embarrassing than she appeared to do. He was not sorry when the bus at last rolled into the market square of Porvoo and began to disgorge its passengers.

There were some fine old buildings

flanking the square, stalls on the cobblestones, and people sitting under the trees, but they had scarcely had time to take all this in when a man elbowed his way through the crowd and planted himself in front of them.

'I am Esko,' he said. 'Come with me.'

Without further introduction he took the girl's suitcase and started walking away. Brady was about to make some protest but saw that Linda was accompanying the man without any hesitation and decided that it was best to do the same.

There was a not very new Ford Corsair parked not far away. Esko opened the boot and stowed Linda's suitcase, then turned to Brady, took his suitcase also, stowed it with the other, and slammed the lid. He opened the rear door and indicated that they should get in.

'Please.'

They got in.

'I suppose you know what you're doing,' Brady said.

'Don't worry. It's all in order,' she assured him.

Esko got in behind the steering-wheel and started the engine. He was about thirty, thick-set and snub-nosed, wearing a leather jacket and denim trousers; from the back his shoulders had a slightly hunched appearance, but that could have been because of the way he crouched over the wheel, gripping it hard with stubby fingers that were tipped with bitten-down nails.

In spite of Linda's assurance Brady was worrying. What proof was there that this man was a friend and not an enemy? He had simply given his name and Linda had accepted it as sufficient evidence of his identity. And how had he known them? Well, perhaps that had been easy; perhaps they had stood out so clearly from the rest of the passengers that he simply could not go wrong. Still, it was not quite the way Brady had imagined these things were done.

Esko drove with a wild abandon, as though he were fleeing from pursuers, which Brady sincerely hoped was not so. The tyres hammered on the cobblestones, screeched as they swung round corners, and gave a final squeal of protest as Esko jammed on the brakes and brought the Corsair to a shuddering halt outside an old wooden house built in the ancient Russian style. Brady decided that Esko probably drove like that, not because he feared pursuit, but because he had once had aspirations to become a rally driver, and perhaps still had; it was something that probably ran in the blood of all Finns.

It was obviously an old part of the town: the street was wide and tree-lined, but there was scarcely any traffic using it. Two blonde girls rode past on bicycles, chattering and laughing; a dog sniffed at one of the trees and cocked up its hind leg; and an elderly man in a trilby hat made his way slowly along the pavement, prodding at the ground with a stick.

'We are here,' Esko said.

He got out and opened the door for them. They got out too and Esko took the suitcases from the boot. The houses were all squarely built with tall windows in ornate frames and heavy drainpipes leading down from the eaves. Linking the houses and presenting a solid front to the street were high wooden fences with doors in them. Esko pushed open the door at the side of the house by which he had stopped the car, led the way down a short passageway, up some steps on the right, through another doorway and into the house. There was a smell of pine and furniture polish, a sense of stepping into the past, on to the set of a Chekov play. Brady almost expected to see an ancient serf stepping forward to take the luggage and lead them to their rooms. But there was only a woman, young, pleasant-featured, smiling a welcome, as though their arrival had been expected — as no doubt it had.

'I hope you had an easy journey,' she said. Her English was good, and it was such a conventional greeting that Brady could have laughed.

But it was Linda who answered: 'Thank you. We have had nothing to complain of.'

Brady wondered whether it was a code,

but rejected the idea. The woman looked too transparently honest for that.

Her name was Sonja. Brady got the impression that she was Esko's wife, though it was not explicitly stated, and there was no mention of any surname.

'I will show you where you sleep. Then perhaps, if you are hungry, you would like a meal.'

It was a large room with a large double bed. Esko dumped the suitcases and went away. He was apparently not a talkative man.

Sonja said: 'There is a bathroom at the end of the passage. Now I will go and prepare the meal.'

She went away too. Brady looked at the bed.

'They think we're married.'

'Naturally,' Linda said.

'It's going to be cosier tonight.'

'It isn't,' she said.

'Are you suggesting we toss for it?'

'I'm suggesting nothing of the kind.' She was being very cool again. 'You can sleep over there.'

It was a settee standing against the

wall. Brady walked over to it and tested it with his hand.

'It's hard.'

'Don't be so fussy,' she said. 'What do you think you're being paid for?'

'For sleeping on that thing I ought to get hard-lying money.'

'You'll be asking for danger money next.'

'And that's not a bad idea either.'

'You'd better take it up with Stewart when we get back.'

'If we get back.'

'Oh, for Pete's sake,' she said, 'why shouldn't we get back?'

'You tell me,' Brady said. 'So far I'm groping in the dark. I don't even know what we're here for.'

But instead of telling him she opened her suitcase and began to unpack.

* * *

It was a good simple meal served in a spacious dining-room with windows looking out on to the quiet street. Sonja waited on them unobtrusively, but there was no sign of Esko, and through the window it was possible to see that the Corsair had gone.

'It looks as if Esko has taken the car away,' Brady said. 'I wonder where he's off to.'

'Probably back to work. He has a job, you know.'

'No, I didn't know. What kind of job? Apart, that is, from meeting people like us, which could hardly be very regular employment.'

She helped herself to salad. 'He's employed at one of the saw-mills. The saw-mill belongs to a man named Jaakko Karsten who owns quite a lot of property around here — including this house.'

'You're beginning to tell me things. Go on like this and you'll soon be taking me into your confidence.'

She toyed with the salad and seemed to be making up her mind whether or not to hand out any more information. Finally she said: 'Perhaps you ought to know — Jaakko Karsten works for us.'

'You mean he's a British Intelligence agent?'

'Not officially, no. The Finns are very sensitive about that kind of activity taking place on their soil. Understandably so; they can't afford to do anything that would damage their relations with the Soviet. And the Russians would take a very dim view of the situation if they were aware of it.'

'A spy on their doorstep, you mean?'

'He's not exactly a spy, though he does send some useful information occasionally. But his work for us is more of this kind.'

'Aiding and abetting?'

'You could call it that.'

'Why does he do it? He can't need the money.'

'That's true. But you must understand that there are people in Finland who still hate the Russians, who have not forgotten the Winter War, the bombing of Helsinki, the dismemberment of their country.'

'And Karsten is one of them?'

'His father was killed in the fighting, his mother in an air-raid; the family estates in Karelia are now part of the U.S.S.R. He has reason for some bitterness.'

It seemed to Brady that she was putting the case with a certain vehemence, almost as though she had a personal interest in the matter.

'Do you know him?'

He thought she looked a shade disconcerted, suddenly aware perhaps that she had been talking too much and giving away more than she had intended.

'I have met him,' she admitted. 'In London.'

'And what is he like?'

She hesitated a moment, and then, with a trace of defiance, it seemed: 'He is a very charming man.'

Brady turned his attention to the food, but he was wondering whether there had perhaps been more to that London meeting than merely a brief encounter, and he felt pretty certain he would get no satisfactory answer to the question even if he asked it. There was no reason why it should have bothered him, but it did; and though he himself had never met Jaakko Karsten and knew only, from what Linda had said, that the Finn was a wealthy and charming man, he was already prepared to dislike him on sight. Or even on no sight at all. So could it be that there was some jealousy creeping in there somewhere? But that was ridiculous. He was not in love with Linda, so why should he care two pins how intimately she had become acquainted with Karsten in London? Why, indeed! And yet he did care. So was he falling a little in love with her after all? Maybe he was. And that was certainly not the wisest of things to do in the circumstances. But when had wisdom ever played much of a part in that sort of operation?

The meal came to an end with no further mention of Jaakko Karsten.

'How are your feet?' Linda asked.

'My feet?'

'Do you feel fit enough to walk a little way?'

'More sight-seeing?'

She nodded. 'More sight-seeing.'

'Okay,' Brady said. 'Let's have a look at Porvoo and to hell with the feet.'

★ ★ ★

68

There was a blue Saab parked on the other side of the road with a man sitting in it and reading a book. Brady had heard that the Finns were a very literate people but it seemed to be carrying literacy a bit far to use parked cars as reading-rooms. The man might, of course, be waiting for someone. Or just killing time. But on the other hand he might be there for a different purpose; he might be doing a bit of surveillance.

'That car,' Brady said.

Linda glanced at him. 'What about it?'

'Why would a man sit in a parked car reading a book?'

'He might like the book.'

'And he might be keeping an eye on things.'

'You are jumpy, aren't you?' she said. But just the same she let him guide her across the street towards the stationary Saab.

Brady made a point of looking in at the man. He was wearing a brown suit which did not seem to fit him very well, and he had a thin, sunken-cheeked face and a long jaw. He was a starved-looking character altogether, with sparse black hair and a high, pale forehead. The book he was reading must have been very absorbing, for he did not glance up from it even though Brady halted by the car and stood there for several seconds peering in at him. Brady tried to read the title of the book, but the man's hand was obscuring it and he could see no more than four or five letters; but what he did see made him feel very little happier; rather the opposite in fact.

Linda had walked on ahead and he hurried to catch up with her.

'Well?' she said. 'Are you satisfied?'

'What do you mean by satisfied?'

'Did he tell you who he was?'

'He didn't say a word. He didn't even look at me. Don't you think that was odd?'

'Not particularly. Why should he look at you?'

'So if you were sitting in a car and somebody came along and took a good look at you through the window you wouldn't even glance back at him?'

'Perhaps it's an interesting book.'

'Oh, it's interesting. At least, I found it so.'

'Don't tell me you read it in half a minute.'

'I read a few letters of the title; that was all I could see.'

'And?'

'They were in Russian script. The Finns don't use that alphabet, do they?'

He could see it had shaken her a little, though she did her best to play it down. 'Lots of Finns understand Russian and probably read Russian books.'

'So do lots of Russians.'

'Forget it, Steve,' she said. 'You'll soon be seeing Reds under all the beds.'

'I certainly mean to look,' Brady said.

After walking for a time they found themselves back at the market square where they had left the bus. It was a pleasantly warm afternoon and people were sitting on the public seats under the trees. Brady kept turning to look for the Saab.

'You think he may be following us?' Linda asked.

71

'I think somebody could be.'

'You imagine things,' she said. 'Let's take a look at the Town Hall.'

It was coral-pink with a leaded roof and a bell turret. It had been built in 1764 in the Swedish style, which to Brady looked much like Georgian English. There was a seat on the cobblestones in front and an old man in a cloth cap was sitting on it and staring fixedly at the main entrance. It looked as though it might have been his daily occupation.

'Very nice,' Brady said. 'Where do we go now?'

They went to look at the Lutheran cathedral which dominated the town from its hill-top site. It was 15th century Gothic. Brady thought it was very nice too.

'Is that all you can say?'

'What did you expect me to say?'

'Something rather more original perhaps. Or would that be expecting too much?'

'I'm sorry,' Brady said, 'but the fact is my mind is distracted by other matters and my feet are beginning to kill me again.'

'If I'd known you had such soft feet I wouldn't have recommended you for the job.'

'And if I hadn't had such a soft head maybe I wouldn't have accepted it.'

When they returned to the house the Saab had gone.

'He must have finished the book,' Brady said.

'Did you think he'd still be here?'

'I don't know what to think. Have you any plans for tomorrow?'

'It rather depends on Jaakko,' she said. 'I expect he'll be making contact.'

They went to bed early; there seemed to be little else to do. Karsten had not yet made contact and the Saab had not returned.

Linda used the bathroom first. When she came back Brady went. It was not quite in the same style as the one in the Helsinki hotel, but there was plenty of space in it and all the necessary equipment. He took his time and when he went back to the bedroom he found that Linda had made a bed for him on the settee.

'So you haven't changed your mind?'

'Did you suppose I would?'

'It was just a happy thought.'

'You'll sleep well enough over there.'

'It could give me a rick in the back. I wouldn't be much help to you with a ricked back.'

'And what makes you think you wouldn't get a ricked back if you slept with me?'

He saw that she had a case there. 'So it's to be the settee?'

'It's to be the settee.'

She had got the last word in again.

5

Finnish Heaven

Jaakko Karsten turned up next morning as they were finishing breakfast. Brady, who had been prepared to dislike him on sight, found it difficult to do so. Karsten, as Linda had said, was a very charming man, though certainly not in any effeminate way. He was big, and his hair was so blond it was almost white. Brady judged his age to be a bit on the upper side of forty, but it was hard to tell. He was not at all handsome; the face was too bluntly made for that, and the abnormally large ears made for a certain lack of proportion; but the charm was in his manner, in his attitude; he seemed to exude friendliness like a large, ungainly dog.

Linda introduced Brady to him and he shook hands vigorously. Brady could detect the strength in that hand, and there was an impression of strength in Karsten's entire body; the bulk was there but no trace of softness; he looked like a man who lived hard.

'So you are the husband, Steve.' He used the familiar mode of address at once, as though it were the natural thing to do, and he laughed, making the 'husband' into something of a joke. Brady was not sure that he altogether liked that, but it was impossible to take offence; Karsten had so obviously intended none.

'You had no trouble getting here?'

'No trouble,' Linda said.

'Good, good.'

'But Steve is worried about a Saab.'

Karsten looked at Brady with a questioning lift of the eyebrows. 'A Saab?'

'There was one parked just across the street yesterday. There was a man in it reading a Russian book.'

'Ah, and you think he was watching this house?'

'It seemed a possibility.'

Karsten walked to the window and

peered out. 'No Saab there now.'

'It was nothing,' Linda said. 'Steve has got the jitters.'

Karsten looked puzzled. 'Jitters?'

'He's nervous. He imagines we're being followed all the time.'

'It wasn't imagination in London,' Brady said. 'You could have been killed.'

'What happened in London?' Karsten asked.

'A man tried to push Linda in front of a tube train.'

'We don't know that,' she said quickly. 'It could have been an accident.'

'Tell me about it,' Karsten said.

Brady told him. Karsten seemed perturbed. He did not like the sound of it, and said so. He looked at Linda and shook his head doubtfully.

'We do not wish for anything bad to happen to you.'

'Nothing bad is going to happen to me.'

'That we must sincerely hope; but I would have been happier if they had sent someone else. I do not think it is a job for a girl.'

'A typically male point of view. You think I am not competent?'

'It is not a question of competence. I think it is not suitable you should do it.'

'Of course it's suitable; don't talk such nonsense. And anyway, I have Steve with me.'

'Ah, yes, certainly you have Steve. But I think he does not understand what the hell it is all about. Do you, Steve?'

'I don't understand a thing,' Brady said. 'But I agree with you — they should have sent someone else. Preferably two different people. Do you still think the Saab was not important?'

'I did not ever say I thought it was not important. Perhaps it was, perhaps not. But I think it is time you were out of here.'

'When?' Linda asked.

'There is no reason to delay,' Karsten said. 'As soon as you are ready we can go.'

'We are ready now.'

They left Karsten in the dining-room and went to fetch their luggage. Karsten had said that he would explain to Sonja.

'Another one-night stand,' Brady said. 'Where do we go from here?'

She snapped the catches of her suitcase. 'You'll see.'

She was being communicative again.

★ ★ ★

Karsten's car was a big Citroen and the journey was a good test of that famous springing and the Michelin tyres, for soon after leaving Porvoo they got on to some minor roads which were very rough indeed. Brady could only imagine what they must be like in winter; and winter lasted a long time in Finland. Which was perhaps why Finns were such good rally drivers. Karsten himself might have done well enough in that line, judging by the way he handled the Citroen; he drove at a pace which on that surface was really giving the suspension a hammering. Brady wondered whether he was pushed for time or whether he always drove like that.

Linda was sitting in the front with

Karsten, while Brady had the back seat to himself. From the position of the sun he reckoned, with no great feeling of satisfaction, that they were travelling in a roughly easterly direction. But the direction kept altering as the roads meandered through forests of birch and pine, with sudden glimpses of lake water and beds of reeds and little wooden cabins, and here and there a landing-stage and a boat or two. It was all wonderfully beautiful, and in different circumstances Brady would probably have appreciated the beauty; but somehow he found it difficult to do so because all the time he was wondering just where in hell Karsten was taking them and what was supposed to happen when they got there.

There was not much talking. Now and then Brady glanced back the way they had come, but it was impossible to see any great distance because of the winding nature of the road. Once Linda caught him at it.

'If you're looking for a Saab on the tail, forget it. The way you keep worrying, you'll be a nervous wreck before we've finished.'

'I'm not really bothered about that possibility,' Brady told her. 'It's the likelihood of being a physical wreck that I don't much care for.'

'You see what kind of a hero I married,' Linda remarked to Karsten.

Karsten laughed. 'I think he just kids you. I think maybe he is not so bad when the chips are down.'

'You could be kidding too,' Brady said. But he gave up looking for the Saab.

He had thought the roads were bad enough, but when Karsten took the Citroen off the road and along a track that branched away to the right the going became really tough. The track had pot-holes in it so big you could have buried a pig in them, and it threaded its way between the trees like a contortionist going into the old routine. Even Karsten was forced to cut down on the speed and drive with extra care; but after a mile or so of this rough going they came to the end of the trail and there was just a placid expanse of water ahead.

Karsten stopped the car. 'We get out here.'

Brady thought it was a pretty superfluous remark; these big Citroens might be able to take most things in their stride but he had never heard that they were amphibious.

There was a wooden jetty poking out from the shore into the lake and on one side of the jetty was a low-roofed boathouse. Karsten walked over to the boathouse, took a key from his pocket, unlocked the door and swung it open. The other two had followed him, and Brady could see a small speed-boat.

'You ever try water-skiing?' Karsten asked.

Neither of them had; it was a gap in their education.

'Good sport. Some day maybe we give it a go, eh?'

'It's not really what we're here for,' Linda said.

'True. But what the hell! You got to relax.'

They fetched their luggage from the car while Karsten brought the boat round to the jetty. He had brought a load of provisions from the house in Porvoo and he put them into the boat with the suitcases. The sunlight glinted on the water and occasionally a whisper of breeze sent a shimmer across its surface as though the whole lake were quivering with apprehension. There was an odour of pine and sedge and warm rich mud.

'It's heaven,' Linda said.

Karsten grinned with pleasure. 'A Finnish heaven.'

The speed-boat carved a furrow in the lake and left a wake of foam. There was an island half a mile from the shore, with another jetty and a strip of shingly beach and a small dinghy pulled up clear of the water. A pathway led away from the beach to a timber bungalow half-hidden among the trees. Karsten cut the engine and allowed the speed-boat to drift alongside the jetty, then made it fast with the painter.

'This is all yours, Jaakko?' Linda asked.

'All mine. I am fortunate, you think?'

'Perhaps you deserve it.'

Karsten grinned. 'Oh, most certainly.'

He carried the provisions up the path to the bungalow while Brady and the girl followed with their luggage. The bungalow was bigger than it had appeared from the jetty; it had been built on sloping ground and the nearer end was raised on stilts; there was a solid granite chimney on one side, tapering from a wide base to a narrow top, and that was the only piece of stone-work to be seen. Steps led up to a veranda at the stilted end, and from the veranda it was possible to get a view of the lake and the boathouse in the distance on the far shore. It was all very peaceful. Which was how Brady hoped it would remain.

The bungalow was comfortably furnished. There was a big sitting-room with a vast open fireplace, and there was a kitchen with a lot of modern equipment, including a gas-cooker and a couple of spare bottles of butane gas. There were also three bedrooms and a storeroom which contained an untidy jumble of gear, amongst which Brady noticed wet-suits, water-skis and an out-board motor.

Karsten saw him looking at the motor. 'It fixes on the little boat.'

'Which would be handy if we should want to get off the island when you're gone,' Linda said.

'That is so. But why should you? Everything is here.'

Inevitably there was a sauna; it was separate from the bungalow, a small wooden cabin with a chimney and a fuel store containing a stack of birch logs and some dry twigs for kindling. Karsten explained how to light the stove and pointed out the buckets for fetching the water.

'You have had sauna bath before?'

'No,' Brady said.

'Then you must certainly try it. You beat each other with twigs, you know.' He grinned.

'Nobody beats me with birch twigs,' Linda said.

'But it is the custom. And you scrub each other too. Makes you feel good.'

'I don't care what the custom is,' she said. 'I don't have anyone scrub me either. Any scrubbing that's required I can manage on my own.'

Karsten looked at Brady and grinned again. 'I think maybe she is warning you off.'

'Or you,' Brady said. He had a feeling that that charm of Karsten's could soon wear off — for him at least.

They went back to the bungalow. Karsten seemed in no hurry to leave; possibly he was proposing to stay for lunch. Brady said that if nobody minded he was going to take a look round the island. Apparently nobody did mind.

'Sure,' Karsten said. 'You do just what you like here. You won't annoy the neighbours. We don't have any.'

It was of no great size — about two hundred yards wide and nearly twice as much in length. Practically the whole area was wooded, but it was swampy in parts, especially on the opposite side from that on which the bungalow was built. Brady took his time, thinking that perhaps Karsten would be gone before he got back. But he had heard no sound of the boat, no sound at all except the rustle of leaves and the occasional plop of a fish leaping for a fly.

Half an hour or more had passed before he returned to the bungalow and mounted the steps to the veranda. There was no one in the big sitting-room, but he knew that Karsten had not gone, for he had noticed the speed-boat still tied up to the jetty. He was about to give a call when he heard a kind of muttering, then a scuffling sound, and then Linda's voice, loud and clear.

'No, Jaakko! Don't be a fool! No!'

He heard Jaakko laughing, and it was the kind of laughter he did not like. He heard the bed creak as he walked into the room, and he saw that Karsten had the girl down on the bed and that she was struggling to free herself. Something flared up in Brady, a blending of jealousy and resentment, bursting out in anger.

'Damn you, Jaakko!'

Karsten turned his head and he was getting up when Brady hit him. It was not an accurate blow; it struck Karsten on the shoulder instead of the jaw. But it was delivered in anger and there was a lot of weight behind it, and it knocked him off the bed and on to the floor, where he stayed for a second or two, looking foolish and going red in the face. A moment more and he might have been on his feet and making a rush at Brady, because he was certainly pretty mad about what had happened. But Linda put the stopper on that; she got up quickly before he could make a move and stepped between the two men like a referee parting a couple of boxers.

'Now stop it, both of you! Stop it!'

Karsten got to his feet and he was breathing hard. 'He hit me. He goddamn hit me.'

'I know,' she said. 'And he shouldn't have done that. But you shouldn't have done what you did either.'

'Ah, that.' Karsten looked faintly sheepish. 'It was just fun. No harm in it.'

'I'll accept that. But it was foolish just the same.'

Karsten massaged his shoulder and stared at Brady. 'You hit me, Steve. I don't think I like that.'

'You weren't meant to like it,' Brady said; but he was cooling fast and he could see that he had perhaps acted foolishly too. There had been no need to hit Karsten; it was just that sudden anger boiling up in him that had made him do it.

'I think maybe I should break your arm for that.'

'Do you think it would help?'

'It wouldn't help at all,' Linda said. 'Now let's all be sensible, shall we? Let's all remember there's a job of work to do and not start acting like a lot of children.'

'There was nothing very childish about the way he was acting,' Brady said.

For some reason the remark seemed to touch Karsten's sense of humour, and he laughed. 'You're damn right there. So now we forget it, eh?'

'I'm willing to if you are.'

'Okay,' Karsten said. 'But another time you better hit me harder; you better hit me with a log or something. Else maybe I do break your arm. You remember that.'

'I'll remember it,' Brady said. Karsten might have been joking; his grin said he was. But there was something in his eyes that said he was not. His pride had been hurt; he had been made to look ridiculous in front of the girl, and he was not going to forget that easily.

But it was she who once again had the last word. 'There isn't going to be another time.'

Karsten just grinned. Brady could see that he did not believe it; he believed there was going to be another time — with her.

Brady hoped he was wrong. He found himself liking big Jaakko less and less.

6

Idyll

Karsten decided not to stay for lunch after all. Possibly he thought it the more tactful course, or possibly he had suddenly remembered some urgent business that needed his attention. Brady watched the speed-boat cutting across the lake, then turned and went back into the bungalow.

Linda was in the kitchen; she had not bothered to see Karsten off.

'He's gone,' Brady said.

She was taking things out of one of the cartons of provisions and stowing them away. 'I know. I heard the boat. Why did you hit him?'

'It was an impulse. It made me mad to see what he was doing.'

'I could have handled it.'

'You didn't appear to be doing too well.'

'You're a fool, Steve. You know that, don't you?'

'Yes, I know it. You don't have to tell me it's no business of mine what goes on between you and Jaakko.'

'Nothing goes on between me and Jaakko,' she said with a flash of anger.

'All right, so that's settled.' He picked up an apple and began to eat it.

'If you're hungry we could have lunch.'

'No hurry. When it suits you.' He looked out of the window. There was a bit of rough grass, then the trees; impossible to see more than a dozen yards or so. 'Do you trust him?'

'Jaakko?'

'Who else?'

'In what way? Professionally or sexually?'

'Professionally. We both know he's not to be trusted the other way, don't we?'

'Yes, I trust him. It's necessary anyway; he's making the arrangements.'

'For what?'

'You'll see.'

'There you go again,' he said. 'Withholding information.'

'It wouldn't do you any good to know.

Why don't you just take things as they come?'

He finished eating the apple. 'Is Jaakko married?'

'Not now. His wife died five years ago.'

'Any children?'

'Not that I've heard of.'

'So he's got no ties? Completely unattached.'

'As far as I know.' She looked hard at him. 'Why are you so interested in Jaakko?'

'A natural curiosity.'

'You don't like him, do you?'

'I thought I did at first. Now I'm not so sure.'

'Because of what happened?'

'Not only that. But I won't say it didn't help.'

'Steve,' she said, and she was giving him that hard look again, 'you're not starting up a bout of jealousy, are you?'

He looked straight back at her. 'What do you think?'

She was silent for a while, apparently turning the question over in her mind and examining it from all angles, and he had a feeling that she was not quite sure of herself, which was unusual with her. But finally all she said was: 'I think we'd better have lunch,' and he knew that she had shied away from it.

After lunch Brady suggested that they might take the boat out on to the lake.

'If you like,' she said.

He went to the store-room to get the outboard motor, and he was about to pick it up when he noticed something else — a large-bore double-barrelled shotgun. It was standing in a cupboard, but the cupboard door was slightly ajar and when he stooped to pick up the motor he caught a glimpse of the stock and then of the rest of the gun. He pulled the door open wider and lifted out the gun and saw that it was in first-class condition. No doubt Karsten did a bit of rough shooting occasionally, though he had not mentioned it. Brady broke the gun and peered through the bore: there was a dull gleam of oil on metal. He replaced it in the cupboard and looked for the cartridges. They were on the top shelf, half a dozen cardboard boxes of them. He closed the cupboard door, picked up the motor and went out to the boat.

The stutter of the engine was an alien note in the stillness of the afternoon. Brady steered the boat round to the other side of the island, and there the lake stretched out for about a mile, the shores gradually converging to form a narrowing channel which bored into the forest where the trees threw a deep shadow across it. They reached the limits of the channel, turned and stuttered back to the open lake. Brady stopped the engine and let the boat drift. He took some fishing-gear from the bottom of the boat and began to fish, using bread pellets for bait.

Linda basked in the sunshine, relaxing on cushions brought from the bungalow, watching him.

'Aren't you glad now that you came, Mr. Brady?'

'On that point, Mrs. Brady, I'm still reserving judgement.'

The sun shone, the boat drifted, he caught no fish and had no desire to catch any. The afternoon wore away in a dreaming somnolence.

'Will Jaakko come back today?' Brady asked.

'No,' she said, 'he won't come back today.'

'I'm glad,' Brady said.

He reeled the line in, started the outboard and took the boat round to the other side of the island.

★ ★ ★

'I'm going to light the sauna stove,' Brady said.

'Oh,' she said, with no sign of interest that he could detect. 'Are you?'

'Yes.'

'Well, don't blow yourself up.'

'You wouldn't like to help?'

'Can't you manage it on your own?'

'I imagine so.'

'Then you don't need any help, do you?'

'You mean you don't want to?'

'Not especially.'

'All right,' he said. 'I'll do it myself.'

There was no difficulty about it, it was

a very simple type of stove. He fetched some of the dry birch twigs from the store-shed and an armful of logs and got the fire going with one match; it was more than he had ever managed as a Boy Scout. When the logs were burning well he went back to the bungalow.

'It'll be ready very soon,' he told her.

'Will it?' Still no sign of interest.

'Don't you want to take a sauna bath?'

'I'm not wildly enthusiastic about being steam-cooked.'

'But you can't come to Finland and not take a sauna.'

'I can,' she said.

'All right,' he said. 'Please yourself.' But he was sore about it just the same. After he had gone to the trouble of lighting the stove she might have shown a bit more interest.

★ ★ ★

He was lying on the bottom shelf and beginning to sweat pretty heavily when the door opened and she came in. She

97

was wearing a towelling bath-robe which she must have found in one of the bedrooms and which was far too big for her; it would have been about right for Karsten, which was not surprising, since it probably belonged to him. She gave Brady scarcely a glance but walked straight through to the dressing-room at the far end, and when she reappeared a couple of seconds later she was no longer wearing the bath-robe.

It was the first time he had seen her naked, and he just hoped it would not be the last, because he liked her that way. Without a word she climbed on to the shelf above him and lay down.

'What made you decide to take some steam-cooking after all?' he asked.

'I knew you'd sulk if I didn't.'

'Was that the only reason?'

'Isn't it enough?'

'I'm flattered you should have so much concern for my feelings.'

'I was thinking of myself having to put up with you in a bad mood.'

'Ah,' he said, 'of course.' And then, a little later: 'Would you like me to beat you with birch twigs?'

'Just try it,' she said. 'Just try anything like that, Steve Brady, and see where it gets you.'

He gathered that she was not in favour of the idea. He doubted whether she would have let him scrub her either. It was a pity she had so little respect for the customs of the country.

Suddenly she sat up and her legs came over the side of the shelf, dangling in front of Brady's eyes.

'God,' she said, 'I'm being boiled, really boiled. Now I know what lobsters feel like.'

She climbed down from the shelf and he could see her skin gleaming with moisture. But this time it was little more than a fleeting rear view, for in a moment she had opened the door of the sauna and was gone.

Brady rolled off his shelf and went to the door. She was already half-way to the jetty, running. He began to run too, but she had a good lead and by the time he reached the jetty she was at the far end. He stopped running and watched her poised for the dive, catching his breath in admiration. For an instant she stood there, motionless in the glow of the evening; then her body arched through the air and entered the water with scarcely a splash.

Brady ran to the end of the jetty and dived in too, making rather more of a splash about it. When he came up he could see her twenty yards away, swimming in the direction of the distant boathouse. The water was cool, in sharp contrast to the steaming heat of the sauna; it invigorated him and he began to swim in pursuit of the girl. He caught her about half-way to the far shore; it had been easier than he had expected, and it occurred to him that perhaps she had not been trying very hard. He stretched out his hand and grabbed her left ankle, and she stopped kicking and rolled over in the water, and he caught a glimpse of her breasts as for a moment they appeared above the surface. He released her ankle, and then they were both treading water and he could see her hair clinging to her head like seaweed.

'Were you really trying to get away from me?' he asked.

He thought he detected a hint of laughter in her eyes. 'Wouldn't that be rather hopeless now?'

'And besides,' he said, 'why would my ever-loving wife wish to do such a thing?'

'Some ever-loving wives are dead keen to get away from their ever-loving husbands.'

'But not this one?'

He saw the laughter in her eyes again, but she made no other answer. He reached out and put his hands on her smooth, slippery body and drew her to him. He found her lips and they both forgot about treading water and went under, still clasped tightly together.

They had to break away and come up for air, and as he surfaced Brady thought he caught sight of something over by the boathouse — a car perhaps. But he could not be sure; the light was deteriorating and there were too many trees. Yet it had certainly seemed like a car at first glance, though when he tried again to pick it out from the background he was unable to do so.

'What are you looking at?' she asked.

'I thought I saw a car.'

'Not that Saab again! Don't you think it's getting to be an obsession with you?'

'I didn't say it was a Saab. Do you think I could tell from here? I just said a car.'

She looked in the direction of the boathouse. 'I can't see anything. Can you still see it?'

'Not now. It was just a momentary glimpse as I came up. It could have been a trick of the light.'

'It probably was. There's nothing over there but the boathouse and the jetty. I'm going back to the house.'

She began to swim. Brady cast one more searching glance at the shore, then turned and followed her. But the chill of the water no longer felt invigorating; it felt merely cold and depressing.

★ ★ ★

They lit a fire in the wide fireplace to combat the evening coolness that had crept in with the lengthening shadows. They had supper on the vast fur hearthrug, not bothering to light the lamps but letting the flames from the birch logs provide a flickering illumination.

Karsten had even been thoughtful enough to provide wine. They clinked glasses and drank, gazing into each other's eyes. The girl's hair had dried and she had brushed it back into submission. She was wearing the towelling bath-robe again; it was bundled round her like an Arab's burnous, her bare feet and ankles protruding enticingly. Looking at her, Brady had the odd idea that her mind had drifted away from the business that had brought her to Finland. He doubted whether Cobb would have approved, but to hell with Cobb.

'It's getting to be more like a real honymoon caper every minute,' he said.

There was a smile twitching the corners of her mouth and he had a feeling that the wine was having some effect. 'I do believe you're getting ideas, Mr. Brady.'

'I've always had ideas, Mrs. Brady, but this time I think maybe you're getting them too.'

She did not deny it.

'We've a choice of three bedrooms,' Brady said.

She drank some more of Karsten's excellent wine and sighed ecstatically. 'Such luxury should be reserved for only the most deserving cases.'

'We are the most deserving cases,' he said.

She did not deny that either.

Later, when they had made the choice of bedrooms and had climbed into one of the big double beds with which the bungalow was provided, it became even more like a real honeymoon caper, and for the first time Brady began to feel glad he had taken the job after all. But for that niggling doubt about the Saab and one or two other small matters which might not turn out to be quite so small when the final count was taken, everything would have been just about perfect. But of course it was not going to stay like this; they had not been sent all the way to Finland at the British tax-payers' expense just so that they could drink Jaakko Karsten's wine and make love in one of Jaakko's magnificent double beds. He was still pretty much in the dark regarding what they had been sent there for, but he was dead certain it was not for that. Which was rather a pity when you came to think about it. It could have turned into a very enjoyable vacation now that his relationship with Linda Manning had really begun to warm up.

He became drowsily aware that she was saying something.

'What?' he murmured. 'What did you say?'

'That woman in Holland.'

'What woman in Holland?'

'You know, Steve; the one you were going round with.'

'I wouldn't have said I was going round with any woman. I was doing a job for you, remember? I was putting my life in jeopardy for the sake of Queen and Country.'

'You were putting your life in jeopardy

because you were having your arm twisted.'

'There was that too,' he admitted. 'And I suppose the woman you're talking about is Suze van Linden.'

'Oh, was that her name? I'd forgotten.'

Like hell she had, Brady thought. And he wondered just what all this was leading up to.

'So what about her?'

She was silent for a bit, and he could feel her fingers moving on his chest and giving the hairs a little tug now and then as though to test their strength. Then she said:

'Were you in love with her?'

So that was it — a slice of interrogation on the emotional front. Next thing she would be asking him to fill in a questionnaire.

'I liked her,' he said, choosing his words carefully because this was tricky country. 'And I think she saved my life. I suppose you could say I liked her a lot.'

'But were you in love with her?' She gave a sharper tug at the hair, perhaps to show him that she would tolerate no evasions.

'No,' Brady said, 'I wasn't in love with her.'

She gave a sigh and released the hair, and the palm of her hand began to make caressing movements instead.

'Are you in love with me, Steve?'

He had been waiting for that, but he was still not ready to answer it. He was not, in fact, certain what the correct answer would have been.

'Now there,' he said, 'you have quite a question.'

She waited a while, as though thinking that he might add a bit more, but when he did not she said musingly: 'We ought not to go falling in love with each other, did we?'

'You think not?'

'It would be very unprofessional.'

'I'm not a professional.'

'Temporarily you are.'

'Well, maybe you're right.'

He thought she was going to leave it at that, but it was not to be so.

'All the same,' she said after an

interval during which she had perhaps been turning the matter over in her mind, 'there's no reason why we shouldn't love each other, is there, Steve?'

'That's different from being in love?'

'Oh, much different.'

It was a nice distinction, but if it soothed her professional conscience it was all right with him. But maybe she was simply laughing at him anyway. And certainly she was laughing, or rather chuckling softly; though when he asked her what she found so amusing all she said was that she was thinking of Stewart Cobb.

'Cobb?'

'You'll never believe this, Steve darling, but he gave me strict instructions to avoid anything in the nature of extra-curricular activities.'

'That was his expression?'

'Yes.'

'It bloody well sounds like him.'

'I can just picture his face,' she said, and she began to laugh again.

Brady could also picture Cobb's face, frigidly disapproving, and it made him laugh too. So for a time they both laughed together, enjoying the shared thought of Cobb's face.

'It was pretty high-handed of him, dishing out orders like that. Who does he think he is?'

'Frankly,' she said, 'I believe he thinks he's God, but he isn't, you know.'

'You're quite sure of that?'

'Yes,' she said. 'That's a couple of steps higher up the ladder. And anyway it's none of his damned business what we do together as long as it's not prejudicial to the proper carrying out of the allotted task, is it?'

'I'm with you there all the way. And incidentally, regarding that allotted task, I've been meaning to ask you — '

'You have asked me, and the answer's still the same.'

'Wait and see?'

'Yes.'

'Well,' he said, 'at least there's something nice to occupy the time while we're waiting.'

7

Disturbance

It was about three in the morning when Brady heard the sound of the boat. The engine must have been throttled well back, since it was making very little noise, and if he had not already been awake he doubted whether it would have roused him. Linda was breathing evenly and not making any movement, so it seemed that no motor-boat engine was disturbing her dreams. He thought about waking her but decided not to.

The sound grew slightly in volume, apparently drawing nearer to the island; then abruptly it ceased altogether and Brady concluded that the boat had reached the jetty. His immediate thought was that Jaakko Karsten had returned, and he was none too pleased about it. Why the devil did he have to come back in the middle of the night? He might at least have waited a few more hours and arrived at a more reasonable time.

But then it occurred to Brady that perhaps it was not Karsten, that perhaps it was someone who had broken into the boathouse and borrowed the speed-boat without bothering about any trivial formalities like asking permission from the owner. And he was even less happy with that possibility than he had been with the first.

Taking care not to wake the girl, he slid out of the bed, dragged on a pair of trousers, and with his bare feet making no sound on the floor, crept silently out of the room. It was not dark; there was a kind of grey twilight which made everything look cold and dead. Brady, without a shirt, felt a little cold himself, and a bit scared into the bargain if the truth were told. He even had an inclination to go back and rouse Linda Manning, because, after all, she was the professional while he was just somebody who had been roped in to help with the chores. But the Brady pride, such as it was, stopped him from doing anything quite so spineless and instead he opened the door of the store-room, took the shotgun out of the cupboard and slipped a couple of cartridges into the breech.

He had heard no sound since the engine of the boat had cut out, and he was thinking that it was certainly not Karsten who had arrived in it, since he would have been walking into the bungalow by this time, all jolly and friendly and hail-fellow-well-met even if it was only three o'clock in the morning. But nobody had walked in, friendly or unfriendly, so maybe it would not be a bad idea to take a few steps and see just what in hell was going on outside.

Brady took a few steps and got himself into the kitchen, where there was a door which opened out of the rear end of the bungalow. He slid the bolt back and cautiously opened the door, and the first thing he noticed was how cold the night air felt on his bare skin; he could feel the goose-flesh rising all over his chest, but it was hardly the moment to go back and hunt around for a shirt, and he pulled the door open a few more inches and slipped out through the gap and closed it very carefully behind him.

He was on the higher part of the sloping ground on which the bungalow had been built, and there was a path leading off at right angles towards the pump which provided the drinking water. He could just see the pump, and if he had not known what it was he might have thought it was a man standing there. Even so, the first glimpse of it gave him quite a turn and set his heart jumping for a few moments before he realised that what he was seeing was nothing but a pump. He was holding the shotgun in both hands and he began to move warily along the side of the bungalow; which was all right where the grass was thick, but there were some patches of stony ground which got to work on the soles of his feet and were a severe test of his self-control.

When he came to the part where the bungalow was up on stilts he decided to use some cover, and he ducked under the flooring and crept forward until he reached the veranda. He stopped there and looked down towards the jetty, and he could see the speed-boat alongside it, but there was no sign of anyone nearby or on the path leading up to the bungalow. He did not care for that: he would have preferred to have whoever it was who had come over in the boat clearly in sight, and the very fact that no one was in sight indicated that the visit was of no innocent variety. Not that he really needed any further evidence on that point.

Where the devil was the man? Had he taken advantage of Brady's tardiness in coming out of the bungalow and got himself under cover of the trees? And was he even now creeping round to the back door which had been left so conveniently unbolted? It seemed a distinct and unwelcome possibility.

Brady thought of retracing his steps in order to cut off that line of approach before it was too late, but he had scarcely begun to move when he heard a sound which brought him to a halt and set his heart beating again in double-quick time. The sound was a faint cough which seemed to come from some point almost directly above his head, and there could be only one explanation for that — the new arrival was standing on the veranda, probably just at the top of the steps.

Then there was another sound — of a match scraping on a box — and a moment later Brady caught the scent of cigarette smoke. The man was cool, no doubt about that, if at such a time he could pause to enjoy a cigarette.

Brady wondered what line of action to take. There would not have been much point in yelling up through the boards with a demand to know who the man was and what the devil he thought he was doing there? That would simply be to put himself at a disadvantage. Instead, he began to edge away to his right until he had got himself clear of the overhanging veranda; then, holding the gun ready, he took a step or two into the open until he could get a sight of the man above.

The man had one hand on the wooden rail at the top of the steps and his back was turned towards Brady. He appeared to be looking at the door of the bungalow and was possibly figuring out just how to set about getting it open, though he seemed to be in no hurry. No doubt he felt secure enough, since no one else was going to come out to the island now that he had taken the boat; but he was a cool customer nevertheless.

Brady watched him, while the man smoked away at his cigarette unconcernedly. The air was still but chilly, and the goose-flesh was turning Brady's skin into a pretty good imitation of a nutmeg grater. He could smell the smoke of the cigarette and the scent of the pines and the muddy, water-weedy odour coming up from the lake; he could smell, too, the oil on the shotgun, pungent and slightly bitter, like the smell of an armourer's shop.

Suddenly the man made a move: he dropped the butt of the cigarette and ground it under his foot. Then he started towards the door.

'Hold it.' Brady said; and he brought the shotgun up and pointed it at the man.

The man turned, not fast, still taking it coolly, until he was facing Brady; then he stood perfectly motionless with hands hanging at his sides, taking care not to make any move that might trigger off the gun.

Brady took a step closer, staring up at the man and trying to get a clearer view of his features. It could have been the one who had sat reading a book in the Saab in Porvoo, but in that light it was impossible to be certain.

'Who are you?'

He got no answer to that.

'What are you doing here?'

He thought for a moment that he was going to get no answer again, but suddenly the man said:

'Look, why not put the gun down? You could kill somebody. You know that?'

He had a harsh voice and a neutral kind of accent, difficult to place.

'I could kill you,' Brady said.

The man laughed. 'That's what I meant.'

'So now are you going to tell me why you're here?'

'It could turn out to be a long story.'

'I've got the time.'

'You'll get cold,' the man said. 'Why don't we go inside?'

Brady thought it over. The man was right about getting cold; it was not just the goose-flesh now; he was shivering so much he could hardly keep the gun steady. It would be warmer inside the bungalow, and he could wake Linda and get her advice on how to handle a situation which seemed to be getting a bit beyond him. It was all very well to threaten a man with a shotgun, but there came a time when you had to move on from there; you could not hold the position indefinitely like figures in a tableau vivant; it tended to become a trifle rigid.

'All right,' he said, 'but it'll have to be the back way; that door is locked.'

The man walked to the steps and began to descend. Brady watched him closely until he reached the ground.

'You go on ahead. And take it slowly.'

The man obeyed instructions; he obviously had a healthy respect for the shotgun. Brady kept him in sight as they turned the corner of the bungalow and climbed the slope to the back door. When he reached the door the man stopped.

'Open it,' Brady said.

The man tried the handle. 'It's locked.'

'It can't be. I came out that way.'

'It's locked now,' the man said.

'I tell you it can't be. Try it again.'

The man tried it again. 'It's either locked or bolted. See for yourself if you don't believe me.'

Brady sensed a trick. Only Linda could have re-bolted the door, and it was hardly likely that, having awakened and found him gone, she would have made her way to the kitchen and without further investigation have bolted the door. It simply made no sense. But the door might have become jammed somehow and there was only one way of finding out.

'Stand back then,' he said, and he made a warning gesture with the barrel of the gun. 'Don't get any bright ideas about jumping me.'

'I'm not getting any bright ideas,' the man said; and to prove it he took about four paces backwards, away from the door.

Brady held the gun in his right hand at hip level, keeping the barrel directed towards the man, while he backed up to the door and groped for the handle with his other hand. He found it, gave it a turn, and leaned on the door. The door resisted; apparently the man had been telling the truth and the door was either bolted or jammed. But he still did not believe that Linda would have bolted it, and how could it have become jammed? So perhaps it merely needed a stronger push. He turned the handle a bit further and leaned back heavily on the door; and it must have been the catch that had not been fully released the first time, for the door suddenly gave way easily under his weight and he staggered back, his heel striking the step and throwing him off balance.

The man came at him quickly then, allowing him no time to recover. His right foot shot out and the toe caught Brady on the side of the jaw when he was about half-way down. Brady went down completely and he thought his head had exploded, though in fact it was one barrel of the shotgun going off as his finger closed involuntarily on the trigger.

He lay on his back for a while, dazed and shaken, and he was expecting the man to come at him again and finish the job, but nothing happened. He had dropped the gun as it fired, and when he sat up and got his vision back to something like normal he could see no sign of his attacker. Which proved one thing: the discharge from the shotgun had certainly not hit him.

Brady got to his feet, picked up the gun and ran along the side of the bungalow until he could get a view of the jetty; and it was as he had expected: the man was already casting off the painter of the speed-boat. A moment later he had stepped into the boat and started the engine.

Brady, who had paused at the angle of the veranda, began to run again, shouting at the man to stop. If he had given half a second's thought to the matter he would have realised that such an order was hardly likely to have much effect and that he was merely wasting his breath. The boat began to move away from the jetty and Brady felt all the blind anger of a frustrated man who had also taken a kick on the jaw and was not at all sure that he would be in any condition to eat a solid breakfast. In his rage he stopped running, raised the butt of the shotgun to his shoulder, and fired the second barrel in the general direction of the receding speed-boat.

It was more a gesture of ill-will than anything else, and he had little expectation at that range of achieving any tangible result. He was surprised, therefore, to hear a faint cry just audible above the sound of the boat's engine, and he could not be absolutely certain that he had not imagined it. And even if he had not, it must have been no more than an involuntary reaction to the sharp sting of an almost spent shot, in the neck or on the hand perhaps, inflicting a little momentary pain but nothing more.

'Damn you!' he muttered vindictively.

'Damn you, you bastard!'

He turned and began to walk back to the bungalow. Half-way there he met Linda Manning.

She looked at him with raised eyebrows. 'Have you gone crazy?' she asked.

He felt pretty sore at that kind of remark coming from her. He might have been killed and she had done nothing to help him. He ignored the fact that it was his own fault for not having wakened her.

'What do you mean, have I gone crazy?'

'Firing off guns in the middle of the night with no shirt on. Doesn't that seem crazy to you?'

'Not when there's a man trying to break into the bungalow, it doesn't.'

'What man? I don't see any man.'

'Of course you don't see him. He got away. Surely you heard the boat.'

She had to admit that she had heard it. 'You mean somebody used Jaakko's boat to come out here?'

'That's it.'

'Why did you shoot at him?'

'He kicked me on the jaw, that's why.'

'Do you know what he wanted?'

'No, I don't. Except that he wanted to get into the bungalow.'

'Did you speak to him?'

'Yes, I spoke to him.'

'And he answered?'

'Yes.'

'So he spoke English?'

'Yes.'

'Was he the man in the Saab?'

'I don't know; I didn't see him any too clearly. He could have been.'

She gazed out across the twilit lake. There was no sound of the speed-boat now; it was all very still and quiet.

'I think we'd better go back inside,' she said. 'I'll make some coffee.'

They went into the kitchen and Brady lit the lamp. There was a pattern of holes in the lintel above the door, as though woodworm had been at work.

'That's where the first barrel-load went,' Brady said.

She looked at the marks. 'Not very accurate shooting if you were aiming at a man.'

'It was an accident. I tripped over the step and then the swine kicked me and the gun went off.'

'You're going to have a bruise,' she said, examining his jaw. 'Can you move it freely?'

Brady worked the jaw. It hurt a bit, but not badly, and there were no creaking sounds.

'Nothing broken.'

She began to make the coffee. 'Why on earth didn't you wake me at once?'

'I didn't like to bother you?'

'Idiot!'

'Well, I didn't know who it was, did I? I just heard the boat. It could have been Jaakko.'

'Coming back at this hour! Did you really think that was likely?'

'No,' Brady admitted, 'I didn't think it was likely.'

'And that's why you got the gun?'

'That's why I got the gun.'

She handed him a cup of coffee. 'Next time don't take so much on yourself. Wake me at once.'

'You think there'll be a next time?'

'What's happened once can always happen again.'

Brady drank some coffee. 'Linda, my sweet,' he said, 'let's go home.'

She gave him one of her cold looks. 'You're being pusillanimous again.'

'I know. It's the way I feel.'

'Well, you'd better snap out of it. You've got some money to earn and we're not going home until you've earned it.'

'You're a mean slave-driver,' Brady said. 'But where's the sense of going on with the thing now? It's perfectly obvious that they're on to us.'

'It's perfectly obvious that who are on to us?'

'I don't know. Whoever they are.'

'Why is it obvious?'

'Because of that man, that's why. Why else would he have come out here?'

'He could have been a common thief who thought the place was deserted.'

'Do you believe that?'

She made some play with her coffee-cup but did not answer the question.

'There was nothing common about

him,' Brady said. 'And I think you know what he was after. So why don't you tell me?'

'What good would it do you?'

'It would relieve my curiosity.'

'And it might bring on another attack of pusillanimity.'

'In that case maybe you'd better not tell me.'

'I had no intention of doing so,' she said.

She was a great one for setting your mind at rest.

8

Wilkins

Karsten arrived half-way through the morning with the news that someone had broken the lock on his boat-house.

'We know,' Brady told him. 'We had a visitor during the night.'

Karsten noticed the bruise on Brady's face. 'You had a fight?'

Brady thought he sounded fairly happy with the idea. Could be he was still harbouring a grudge.

'A very brief one. He kicked me and I took a shot at him with your gun.'

'You hit him?'

'Is there any blood on your boat?'

They were standing on the jetty. Karsten looked down at the boat. 'I don't see any.'

'Then I doubt whether I hurt him much even if I did hit him.'

'Do you know who he was?'

'I can't be certain, but he could have been the man who was in the Saab in Porvoo.'

'He could have been anybody,' Linda said. Karsten looked at her. 'Did you see him?'

'No.'

'But you don't think he was the man with the Saab?'

'I think it would be jumping to conclusions to suppose he was.'

'It seems a pretty natural conclusion to me,' Brady said. He turned to Karsten. 'They're on to us, you know.'

'Who are?' Karsten asked.

'Oh, for God's sake!' Brady said. 'Are you taking that line too?'

For answer Karsten suggested that they should go up to the bungalow and give him the whole story. They did that, and he listened with interest, frowning slightly from time to time. He made no comment, but he looked very thoughtful when the account was finished.

'I think we should cancel the whole operation right here and now,' Brady said. 'I thing we should go back to Helsinki and grab the next plane for London.'

Karsten nodded. 'That would be one way of finishing the job. It might not accomplish much but it would certainly finish it.'

'It's out of the question,' Linda said.

'You intend to go on with it?'

'Of course.'

'It might be dangerous.'

'That's a possibility which has to be accepted.'

'Oh, fine,' Brady said. 'Just fine. What's a bit of danger between friends?'

'You knew it wouldn't be without a degree of risk when you took it on.'

'That's true. And there was a little voice inside me saying don't touch it, Steve; don't touch it with a barge-pole. I should have listened to that little voice. I shouldn't even have touched it with a ruddy great barge, let alone the pole.'

'But greed overcame faint-heartedness, didn't it?'

'That's a nasty way of putting it.'

'How would you put it?'

'Necessity overcoming prudence.'

'All right, we'll accept that. But either

way, you're in it now and you're not wriggling out just because somebody kicked you on the jaw.' She spoke to Karsten. 'You've set everything up?'

'Everything,' Karsten said. 'Esko is waiting at the boathouse with the Volvo. You can take it whenever you please.'

'We'll leave today then.'

'Where are we going this time?' Brady asked.

She turned on him one of her most bewitching smiles. 'Why, Russia of course. Didn't I tell you?'

'I knew it,' Brady said. It had been leading up to this right from the start but he had tried to close his eyes to it. Now he could do so no longer. 'I bloody well knew it.'

She smiled again, even more bewitchingly. 'It's all part of the honeymoon caper, Steve darling. You'll love it, you really will.'

★ ★ ★

Karsten ferried them across to the boathouse in the speed-boat. There

131

were two cars — the Citroen and a Volvo Estate with a lot of what looked like camping gear stowed in the back. Esko was sitting in the Volvo and smoking a pipe, but he got out when the boat arrived.

'Is he going with us?' Brady asked.

Karsten shook his head. 'He came along to drive the Volvo. I'll be taking him back in the Citroen.'

'Who does the Volvo belong to?'

'It's hired in your name. I've brought the documents for you to sign.'

'So now I have to start signing things.'

'It's just routine,' Linda said.

'That's what it all is, isn't it? Some routine!'

Karsten got the documents out of the Citroen and Brady signed them. The name of the hire firm meant nothing to him; he assumed it was a Finnish concern and he wondered if Karsten had a finger in it. Taking all things into consideration, he thought it more than likely.

'Who drives?'

'You'd better,' Linda said. 'It will look more natural.'

'I don't know the way to Russia.'

'Just keep heading east,' Karsten said, and he gave a laugh. 'You can't miss it.'

Brady was not amused.

'There's a road map in the car,' Linda said. 'I'll navigate.'

He saw that there was no way out of it, it had, of course, all been arranged before they left England, only he had not been trusted with the details. Cobb had known and Linda had known, but they had not told him because they had thought it might scare him off. And they had been right; too true, they had. But it was too late now; he was in it, in it up to the neck.

He stowed the luggage with the camping gear in the back of the Volvo and then got in behind the wheel. Linda was in the other seat studying the map. Karsten peered in at them, grinning.

'Happy landings.'

Brady wondered sourly where he had picked up that expression. He decided that it was not really necessary to thank Karsten for his hospitality.

'We'll be seeing you, Jaakko,' Linda said.

'Sure — on the way back.'

So he thought they were coming back. Or maybe he was just looking on the bright side of things for their benefit. It was easy for him.

Brady started the engine, and the last thing he saw in the mirror as he drove away from the boathouse was Esko placidly smoking his pipe and watching without any discernible expression the receding tail of the Volvo.

Lucky Esko.

★ ★ ★

It was late in the afternoon when they reached the Russian border post. Brady felt like a criminal about to be interviewed by the police, and it must have been showing enough for Linda to notice.

'Why don't you relax?' she said. 'There's nothing to worry about. We're just an ordinary married couple on a camping holiday.'

'You think they'll believe that?'

'There's not the slightest reason why they shouldn't.'

'I can think of plenty of reasons.'

'Forget it. And let me do the talking.'

He glanced at her in surprise. 'You speak Russian?'

'I had a crash course.'

It was something else she had not bothered to tell him. And she might have used a happier expression than crash course; it had a certain ring to it that was not altogether encouraging. They could both be on a crash course right at this very moment.

Passing through just ahead of them were a couple of Land-Rovers and a minibus which appeared to be travelling in convoy. There were a lot of young people in a variety of rather garish clothing milling around them and causing a certain amount of confusion which the Russian officials seemed to be doing their best to sort out. An older man, who could have been the leader of the party, strolled back to the Volvo, rested a hand on the roof and spoke through the open window on the driving side.

'I'm sorry,' Brady said. 'I'm afraid I don't understand.'

The man grinned. 'Ah, you're English. The Finnish registration fooled me.'

He was about six feet tall and as thin as a wire nail — a rather bent wire nail. He had a concave outline from the waist to the chin, a long face and skimpy brown hair untidily scattered over a scalp that showed through here and there in sun-tanned patches. His teeth were large and prominent, and he had a high-pitched, neighing sort of voice that seemed to go well with the rest of him. He looked about forty.

'Yes,' Brady said, 'we're English.'

'Jolly good show. My name's Wilkins. For my sins I act as senior courier, guide and general dogsbody to rabbles such as this.' He indicated with a sweep of his hand the young people just ahead. 'Afraid we may delay you a bit. Russians are sticklers for all the formalities. In their nature, I suppose. Didn't catch your name.'

Brady was about to tell Wilkins that he had not mentioned his name and saw no reason why he should when Linda chipped in.

'Brady. Mr. and Mrs. Stephen Brady.'

'How do you do?' Wilkins said, and he pushed a long bony hand on the end of a long bony arm through the window. There was no alternative but to shake it, otherwise it might have been left dangling there indefinitely. They did so and he withdrew it, but his gaze lingered for quite a while on Linda before he turned again to Brady. 'I congratulate you. Your wife is charming, quite charming.'

'Well, thank you,' Linda said.

Brady said nothing. He waited for Wilkins to go away, but the man seemed to be in no hurry to do so. His eye was caught by the camping gear in the back of the Volvo.

'So you're on a camping holiday too?'

Brady admitted that that was the intention.

'Your first time in Russia?'

'Yes,' Brady said, and he wondered just how you got rid of a pest like Wilkins, short of being down-right rude.

'Then you really must let me help you,'

Wilkins said. 'I know all the ropes, you see. There's a camping site on this side of Leningrad which I suggest you make your target for tonight. I'm taking my crowd there and you can follow us. We'll wait for you until you're through with the customs and whatnot. Right?'

'There's no need — ' Brady began; but once again Linda chipped in.

'I think that would be a marvellous idea. Thank you, Mr. Wilkins. It's very kind of you.'

'Not at all,' Wilkins said. 'And do call me Charles. Everyone else does. Oh, and by the way, you can get petrol coupons at the Intourist office. They'll try to arrange everything for you, but just tell them you're tagging along with my lot.'

He sheered off after that and walked ahead to join his party. Brady could see him answering questions, bending over like a human lamp-standard and gesturing with his hands.

'Interfering idiot. Why is it that some people can't resist poking their noses into other people's business?'

'Now, Steve,' Linda said, 'you mustn't

138

be so ungrateful. He was only trying to help.'

'We don't need his help.'

'It won't do any harm to accept it. Tacking on to his safari might not be at all a bad plan. It'll serve as camouflage.'

'So you think we need camouflage?'

'Whether we need it or not, we may as well accept what the gods provide.'

'Okay then,' Brady said. 'If the gods provided us with Wilkins we'd better not throw him back in their teeth.'

'Now you're being sensible,' she said.

He was on edge all the time they were held up at the checkpoint. He was afraid something would be found wrong with the passports and the International Driving Permit, that the Volvo would be suspect and that his bogus relationship with Linda Manning would be instantly recognised. His fears, however, were groundless; the officials were friendly and courteous, and though they made a thorough examination of the luggage and the car, they did so as though it were merely routine and not as though they expected to find anything out of order.

Finally, with the formalities completed, the Volvo and its occupants were allowed to proceed on their way.

Wilkins and his convoy were waiting for them further up the road. He held up his hand and Brady brought the Volvo to a halt. Wilkins came to the window.

'No trouble?'

'No trouble,' Brady said. 'Did you think there would be?'

'You never can tell. They can be a bit sticky at times. Red tape, you know.' Wilkins gave a neighing laugh and Brady gathered that this was meant to be a joke. He found it difficult to echo the laughter; it was all very well for Wilkins, he was safe enough going about his perfectly legal business of conducting a pack of innocent young tourists into Russia; he had nothing to feel guilty about. Brady, on the other hand, felt as guilty as hell; and it was no use Linda telling him to relax, because he was not going to feel really relaxed until they were out of Russia and on the flight home. And when that would be he had no idea, no idea at all.

'Well, then,' Wilkins said, 'I suppose we'd better be on our way. Just hang on to my tail, old man, and you can't go wrong.'

He ambled away to rejoin his own party, walking with a disjointed, unco-ordinated kind of gait, climbed into one of the Land-Rovers and started the engine. A few moments later the convoy was in motion.

Brady got the Volvo moving too. 'I really believe he expected us to have trouble getting through.'

'Nonsense,' Linda said. 'Why should he?'

'I don't know. Maybe we just look phoney.'

'If we looked phoney how come the Russians let us through so easily?'

'Maybe they're just biding their time. Letting us get well and truly into the trap.'

'What trap?'

'You tell me.'

'There isn't any trap. So why don't you clear all that rubbish out of your mind and enjoy the lovely Russian scenery?'

The lovely Russian scenery looked very much like the lovely Finnish scenery on the other side of the border, only more sinister. At least, so it seemed to Brady. There were forests of pine and birch, and glimpses now and then of placid lake water; and he recalled that before World War Two this had all been part of Finland. But the Finns had pulled up their roots and retreated into what remained of their own country after the carve-up, leaving the Russians to do what they would with their new territory.

The road had a good surface but there were not a great number of private cars using it. They met a few coaches and some heavy lorries, presumably heading for Finland, and Brady wished he were going that way too. He wondered what the devil they were in Russia for, but he knew it would be useless asking; one day no doubt he would know, only then it might be too late. They passed through a few villages and a small town or two, in which there were people going about their business as people did everywhere in the world.

'Looks peaceful,' Brady said.

'Why shouldn't it?'

'So why don't we leave them alone? Why do we have to go spying on them?'

'Why do they have to go spying on us?'

'I don't know. It's a damned silly business all round. You'd think everybody could come to an agreement to call the spies home and save the taxpayers' money.'

'It'll never come to that.'

Brady glanced at her. 'Maybe you wouldn't want it to. You'd be out of a job.'

'I imagine I could find something else to do.'

'Why don't you give it up anyway and marry me for real?'

'On your prospects?'

'With enough incentive I might make a go of things.'

'And I would be enough incentive?'

'Too true, you would.'

'It's sweet of you, Steve,' she said, and she sounded thoughtful. 'I believe you really mean that, don't you?'

'Well, why shouldn't I mean it?'

'Are you proposing to go back to dealing in antiques?'

'I never was very good at that. Maybe I'm too honest.'

'Well,' she said, 'we'll talk about it sometime.'

But he knew she really meant that it was just not on. She was probably right; it was a pleasant dream but no more than that. She would stick to the work she was doing and he would drift out of her life again the way he had after that affair in Holland. And maybe some day she would want his help on another job and would look him up again. But they would both be a bit older then, a bit wiser perhaps, a bit further along the road; so that it would be harder to pick up the threads.

'Yes,' he said, 'we'll talk about it — sometime.'

9

The Late Mr. Koulis

It was a wooded camping site and
there was a fresh scent of pines,
the ground springy underfoot like an
expensive carpet. There was a lake
close by, and lavatories, wash-rooms
and showers, a small restaurant and a
kitchen for those who preferred to do
their own catering. There were also post
and telegraph facilities, and they could
have hired a tent and bedding if they had
not brought their own. There was not a
sign of litter anywhere on the site.

'Tidy people,' Brady said.

'Which is more than you can say of
the British. They'll probably fine you if
you drop any rubbish.'

'I don't intend to. I'm going to be
on my best behaviour while I'm in this
country. I'm not expecting it to help
much, but it might count in my favour.'

An official showed them where to park the Volvo and where to pitch their tent. Wilkins strolled over to give them a hand, leaving his party to fend for themselves. The tent that Karsten had supplied was brand new and Brady was wondering just how to set about erecting it, but he would rather have tackled the job without Wilkins's assistance; the man was getting to be something of a leech.

'Ah,' Wilkins said, 'you got this in Finland, I'd say.'

Brady did not bother to answer. He turned his back on Wilkins and began to struggle with the tent.

'I'm afraid you're not doing that quite right, old man,' Wilkins said, after watching him in silence for a while. 'It goes up quite easily when you know how. Let me show you.'

'I can manage,' Brady said.

'Oh, I'm sure you can, but a little help never came amiss, I always say.'

'I said I could manage.'

Linda appeared to sense that he was losing his temper, and she hastened to smooth things over. 'Now, Steve darling,

I'm sure you could use some help. Don't be a bear when Mr. Wilkins is being so kind.'

'Perhaps,' Wilkins said, 'Mr. Brady thinks I'm interfering.'

'But of course you're not interfering. Is he, Steve?'

Brady got the message — treat Wilkins with courtesy. And it might not be such a bad idea at that; he was doing none too well with the tent on his own.

'Well, thanks,' he said, none too graciously. 'It might be easier with two.'

Wilkins had not been idly boasting, he did know how to erect the tent; Brady felt like a rather raw tender-foot being given a lesson by a scoutmaster. When he came to think of it, there was something decidedly scout-masterish about Charles Wilkins; possibly it came from conducting parties of young people on tours of Soviet Russia. He was familiar with the camping site, having been there before.

'If you want to know anything just come and ask Charles. Right?'

'Right,' Brady said; and after that

Wilkins strolled away to see how his youngsters were getting on.

'He's very obliging,' Linda said.

Brady looked at her a shade sourly. 'He's a pest.'

'You're only sore because he knows more about putting tents up than you do.'

'I'm not sore. Anyone can put up a tent.'

'You didn't seem to be doing so well on your own.'

'I was working things out. I'd soon have got the hang of it without his help. And incidentally, if you ask me, he's got his eye on you.'

'Is that what makes you dislike him?'

'I don't dislike him. I just thing he's a busybody.'

'And I think he's a nice friendly helpful person.'

It hardly seemed worth while carrying the argument any further, especially as he was aware that he was merely using Wilkins as an outlet for his feelings of general unease. And the devil of it was that he was still so much in the dark that he could not be certain what there was to be uneasy about. He just knew there was something, and that was enough.

Linda had been studying him with a slightly worried frown on her face. Finally she said: 'You're all tensed up, aren't you? If you don't relax your nerves will be in tatters by the time we get to Moscow. And that isn't going to help much.'

'So we're going to Moscow?'

'You didn't expect to come to Russia and not pay a visit to Moscow, did you?'

'Frankly,' Brady said, 'I didn't expect to come to Russia at all. And if you really want the truth, I wish I hadn't.'

'Let's not go over that again,' she said. 'We're here now and you'd better make the best of it.'

'If there is a best of it.'

★ ★ ★

He found sleep unusually elusive. It could have been the hardness of the ground making itself felt through the padding of the sleeping-bag, but he had slept soundly enough in far more uncomfortable conditions in the past, so it was probably the same old worry gnawing away at him like a rat in the cellar. He looked at the luminous dial of his wristwatch and reckoned that it was about a quarter past two. Linda was sleeping as though she had never a care in the world, not moving and not making a sound, and he felt a bit resentful about that. Why should she be able to sleep when he was lying awake? Damn it, the least she could have done would have been to share his worry instead of going off into dreamland like a five-year-old child and leaving him to fight it out on his own. After all, she was his wife — temporarily.

When he looked at his watch again it was twenty past two. Time was really creeping. Five minutes later he decided to get up and see what was going on outside. Not much was likely to be going on at around half-past two in the morning, but anything was better than just lying there and imagining that

150

something might be.

He wriggled out of the sleeping-bag and pulled on his trousers and shoes and a shirt and a sweater, and the girl did not even stir; she was really away. He unfastened the tent door and crawled outside and let the canvas fall back into place. It was a clear night and there was that kind of eerie twilight which he was getting to know pretty well. There were patches of gauzy mist creeping up from the lake and wandering in and out among the trees like lost ghosts, and the piny odour seemed sharper than it had in the daylight.

There was no one around as far as he could see, which was hardly surprising, since anyone in his right senses would be busy stocking up on the sleep. The tents looked like a lot of miniature houses and there was a kind of low sawing noise which puzzled him for a time until he realised that it was someone snoring. Someone with nothing on his mind, no doubt.

Now that he was out of the tent it occurred to him that he might have done better to stay inside. It was decidedly chilly out there, and what was he going to do? Go for a walk? Take a dip in the lake? He had half a mind to go back in again but decided, since he was up and dressed, that he might as well go over and take a look at the Volvo. So he walked across to the car park, and the first thing he noticed was that the door of the Volvo was open and that a man had his head and shoulders inside.

It gave Brady's nervous system a jolt. He had not really been expecting this. For one thing, the doors had been locked, and that meant that the man must be an expert at opening locked cars; and for another thing, what could there be in the Volvo that would be worth looking for? After all, the border guards had already had a look, and they had found nothing. Which proved what? That perhaps they had not looked hard enough? That perhaps the Volvo was something special as Volvos went, with something special hidden away inside it? Something which Linda had brought from England and had passed on to Karsten so that he could stow it in the car? It seemed a possibility.

Meanwhile there was this man ferreting inside, which was what some people would have called a diabolical liberty, and Brady was not at all sure he would not have called it that himself. His approach had obviously been unheard, his feet making very little sound on the springy turf, and he scarcely paused to think out what course of action to take because he could not have been more incensed if he had caught someone in the act of picking his pocket. He just went straight in, got a grip on the man's shoulders and hauled him out of the car.

The man reacted with a viciousness that took Brady by surprise. He twisted round and put a knee in Brady's groin and followed up with a butt to the stomach that drove him back against the side of Wilkins's minibus, which was parked alongside the Volvo. Brady was hurt, but he was angry too. If he had not been so angry he might have called a halt to hostilities and let his opponent get away, but as it was he stuck out a foot and caught the man's ankle just as he was making off. The move was effective; the man went down heavily, sprawling on his stomach in the space between the parked vehicles, and Brady, ignoring the pain in his groin, dropped on him at once and gave a sharp hand chop to the back of the neck.

But this was a tough customer; some people might have packed it in then, but not this boy; he was still as full of fight as a boa-constrictor that had not been eating too well and had a long empty stomach to fill. Brady was still thinking in terms of keeping him pinned to the ground when he suddenly arched his back and with a rearward withdrawing movement slipped out of the hold and was on his feet again. He was playing it dirty too; Brady had just time to turn when he got a kick on the left shin. An inch or two higher and it might have taken off the knee-cap, and even as it was it inflicted enough pain to stoke up those feelings of intense resentment and ill-will that had been there in considerable quantity from the start.

In normal circumstances Brady would probably have turned all his attention to the injured shin, but the circumstances were very far from being normal, and when the man tried once again to rush past him in an effort to escape he again put all his energy into thwarting the move. This time he tried a little of the dirt himself, and his kick really did catch the knee-cap, and it stopped the man in his tracks. Brady knew he had the advantage, and he moved in quickly and slammed the man hard against the side of the Volvo, adding a punch to the side of the jaw for good measure.

It was the punch that finished it. The man went over sideways and his head struck the edge of the wing mirror. Brady heard the sound of the bone cracking; it was a small sound, too insignificant, one might have thought, to be the herald of anything so extreme, so irreversible, so utterly final, as death. Brady did not believe it. Only when he had kneeled down and felt for the no longer beating pulse, listened for the silenced breathing, for the thumping of the heart within the chest, only then was he convinced that he had indeed killed the man.

And he knew what man it was — the one who had sat in the Saab in Porvoo reading a book with Russian lettering on the cover; he was sure of it. He felt sure, too, that it was the man who had taken Karsten's speed-boat and ferried himself over to the island in the lake, for on his right hand were some unhealed abrasions that could have been inflicted by shot from a sporting gun. And now he was dead and ten times more of a problem than he had ever been when alive. Brady thought of all the possible consequences and felt sick. He was still thinking and still feeling sick when he heard Wilkins's voice.

'Well, now,' Wilkins said, 'you really do seem to have got yourself into a fix, don't you?' He sounded calm, hardly surprised even. For him it might have been almost a daily occurrence.

Brady stood up. He saw that Wilkins was fully dressed, and that seemed strange too at such an hour.

'He is dead, I suppose?'

'Yes,' Brady said. 'He's dead.'

'I'll just check on that. You don't mind, do you? Best to make sure.'

'Go ahead,' Brady said. It seemed a crazy sort of conversation, but everything had gone crazy.

Wilkins got down and did what Brady had done. He came to the same conclusion.

'I'm afraid you're right, old man.'

'He hit his head on the mirror. He'd broken into the car and we had a fight.'

'That's about what I thought. Awkward, of course.'

'That's putting it mildly.'

Wilkins was still kneeling on the ground; he was feeling in the inner pocket of the man's jacket. He drew out a wallet and a passport. With the aid of a pencil torch he examined the passport.

'Know who he is? Or perhaps I should say was.'

'I've no idea,' Brady said. 'Some damned Russian, I suppose.'

'No Russian, this joker. Take a look.'

Brady bent down and looked at the passport. It was an American one, made out in the name of George Koulis. The photograph was that of the dead man, no doubt about that. But to Brady it made no sense at all.

'More and more awkward,' Wilkins said. 'It seems you've killed an American citizen on Russian soil in the act of breaking into a Finnish car of Swedish origin. Rather unusual that.' He still did not sound worried. Brady supposed there was no good reason why he should; he was not involved.

He opened the wallet. There were some roubles inside it, nothing else of interest. Mr. George Koulis had apparently not been the kind of man to carry a lot of personal papers around with him. Perhaps he had anticipated that some day someone might search his pockets.

Wilkins stuffed the wallet and passport back in the pocket where he had found them. He stood up.

'The question now arises — what does one do next?'

'I suppose the police will have to be told,' Brady said. But he spoke without enthusiasm; he could imagine the kind of questions they were likely to ask.

'I don't think that would be at all wise,' Wilkins said. 'In fact I'd go as far as to say it would be very unwise in the circumstances.'

'Why?'

''Cause no end of trouble. They'd really give you a going over. You realise you're in a very sticky situation, don't you?'

'Well, of course I realise it. Do you think I'm an idiot?'

'No, not an idiot. A little hasty perhaps, but then aren't we all at times? And there is, of course, Mrs. Brady to consider. I don't imagine you would want her to be involved in a thing like this, would you?'

'But how can I prevent it? The police are bound to find out.'

'Not necessarily,' Wilkins said. 'Not necessarily at all — if we don't tell them.'

'But the body — '

'Can be disposed of.'

Brady stared at him. Wilkins was certainly cool, as cool as they came. And he spoke with absolute confidence and a strange air of authority. But what seemed even stranger was that he should be taking this responsibility upon himself. He was becoming involved of his own free will.

'Are you proposing to help me dispose of it?'

'That was rather the idea.'

'But why should you get yourself mixed up in this? It's not your trouble.'

'Well, let's put it like this, old man. Here we are, a couple of Englishmen in a foreign country. We've got to stick together, haven't we? Can't let the side down, what? Especially with the little woman over there.' He gave a jerk of his head in the general direction of the tents. 'So now let's get this johnnie to a place where he won't attract so much attention.'

'Where's that?'

'The lake, old man, the lake. Obvious place.'

'Yes,' Brady said, 'I suppose it is.'

'Now, I'd say you're a bit younger and stronger than I am, so you'd better take the shoulders. Mind you don't get any blood on your clothes. We'll clean up round the car when we come back. All right?'

'All right,' Brady said. Wilkins seemed to have taken charge. It all seemed pretty criminal, but what alternative was there? Involvement with the Russian police, grilling, maybe a charge of murder? Anything seemed preferable to that. And, as Wilkins had pointed out, there was Linda to think of.

He stooped and got his hands under Koulis's shoulders. 'All right, let's be on our way.'

Koulis was not a particularly heavy man and the distance to the lake was no more than two or three hundred yards, but by the time they got there Brady was sweating freely. It was not so much the exertion that made him sweat, it was the knowledge that they were carrying a dead body and that someone might suddenly appear and want to know why. But no one did appear. They reached the lake, and there was a small rowing-boat drawn up on a shingly strip of beach with the oars lying in it.

'Convenient,' Wilkins said. 'Let's put him down for a moment.'

They put Koulis down on the shingle and Wilkins hunted round for some small rocks to stuff inside his pockets and under the waistband of his trousers, having first pulled his socks over the bottoms so that the ballast should not fall out.

'Don't want him to become too buoyant, do we?'

He thought of everything. Brady wondered whether he had done this sort of thing before, but it seemed an indelicate question to ask.

'Now,' Wilkins said, 'into the boat with him.'

They lifted Koulis into the boat, heaved it down to the water, and got in.

'Can you row?' Wilkins asked.

'I've done a little.'

'Take the oars then. I'm not much good at it. And head for the centre of the lake.'

Brady put the oars into the rowlocks and began to pull away from the shore. The body lay huddled in the bottom of the boat, and every time he reached forward to begin another stroke he imagined that Koulis was staring up at him with accusation in his eyes.

About ten minutes had passed when Wilkins said: 'All right, this will do.'

Brady stopped rowing and let the boat drift. He could no longer see the shore; they were enveloped in a pale mist, damp and chilling, which laid on everything a thin coating of moisture, descending in tiny droplets like a very fine rain. He shivered, the sweat now cold and clammy on his skin.

'Well, come along,' Wilkins said with some impatience. 'Give me a hand to get him over the side.'

The boat heeled over alarmingly as they got the body up on to the gunwale, threatening to capsize and throw all three of them into the lake; but they let it go and it sank quickly, disappearing beneath the grey water.

'And that,' Wilkins said, 'is, I sincerely

hope, the last we shall ever see of the late Mr. Koulis.'

Brady hoped so too. Koulis was not going to be a very pleasant sight if they ever got round to seeing him again — quite apart from the complications it might cause. He rowed back to the shore and they pulled the boat up on to the shingle where they had found it. There was still no sign of any movement in the camp.

'There's one thing I don't understand,' Brady said. 'How did you come to be up and dressed?'

'Couldn't sleep, old man. Fact is, I get these bouts of insomnia. Nothing to do but get up and walk around. Lucky for you as it happened, wouldn't you say?'

'I'm not grumbling,' Brady said. 'I'm very much obliged to you.' But he still thought it was a remarkable coincidence and he was not at all sure that he accepted the explanation.

'And now,' Wilkins said, 'we'd better go and clean that blood off the car. They've got a thing about dirty cars in this country, you know.'

10

Something to Laugh About

Linda was still asleep when he returned to the tent. It seemed amazing to him that she could have slept serenely on while he had killed a man and, with Wilkin's assistance, had dumped the body in the lake. His nerves were still vibrating from the reaction and he could have used a good stiff drink of vodka to calm them down, but it was hardly the right time to go hunting around for vodka. Even if they sold it in the restaurant, the place was closed and would not be open again for a few more hours.

He wondered whether to let the girl sleep on, but decided that she had better hear the bad news at once, because they were going to have to figure out how this affected their plans; and to his way of thinking it affected them a hell of a lot. Like making them all obsolescent maybe.

He had to shake her twice before she woke, and she was not terribly pleased about it when she saw what time it was. But she was a lot less pleased when he told her what had happened.

'Oh, God,' she said, 'you do get into trouble, don't you?'

'Well, don't blame me,' Brady said, and he was feeling pretty aggrieved at the accusation. 'I was only looking after your interests. Did you want the bastard to ransack the Volvo?'

She must have realised that she had been a little unfair to him, and she stretched out her hand and gave his arm a squeeze. 'I'm sorry, Steve. You've had a rough time. It was lucky Wilkins was around to help you.'

'That's something that puzzles me. Why should he go to all that trouble and get himself involved up to the teeth for somebody he'd never set eyes on until yesterday?'

'He told you, didn't he? A fellow Englishman in a foreign country.'

'Do you believe that?'

'Why not? Anyway, why worry about

it? He helped you, and that's that. Accept it.'

She seemed, Brady thought, to be very ready to skate over Wilkins's part in the affair. She had showed very little surprise concerning it, apparently accepting it as something that any Englishman would have done in similar circumstances. Which it certainly was not; not by a long, long chalk. But he let it drop; there were more important points to discuss.

'So what do we do now?'

'How do you mean — what do we do now?'

'It's a simple enough question, isn't it?'

'And there's a simple enough answer. We do just exactly what we were going to do.'

'You don't think we ought to call it a day now and get out of the country before the Russian coppers fish up Koulis's body and start charging me with murder?'

'Steve darling,' she said, 'you're not thinking straight. Can you imagine anything more likely to arouse suspicion than our turning up at the frontier again just one day after crossing it? We're supposed to be taking a holiday in the U.S.S.R.'

'Some holiday. Besides, if the Russians are on to us anyway, what difference will it make?'

'Who said they were on to us? That was your idea.'

'And still is. Why else would Koulis be prying into the car?'

'Aren't you forgetting something?'

He looked at her. 'Forgetting what?'

'Koulis wasn't a Russian. You said he had an American passport.'

'He was reading a Russian book in Porvoo.'

'That proves nothing. And anyway, can you be absolutely sure it was a Russian book? Koulis sounds like a Greek name. He could have been a naturalised American, couldn't he? And those letters you saw on the cover; don't you think there's a possibility they might have been Greek? There are similarities.'

After thinking it over Brady had to agree that she might be right. And there had been nothing whatever to indicate that Koulis had been working for the Russians; he had simply jumped to that conclusion and taken it as proved. So if Koulis had not been working for them there was nothing to suggest that they had any suspicions regarding Mr. and Mrs. Stephen Brady. Which was a relief certainly, but it still did not explain the activities of the late Mr. George Koulis.

'What was he up to then? Why was he tailing us?'

'I don't know. He could have been a free-lance agent with a sharp nose, but I doubt that. It's far more likely he was working for our Nato partners.'

'You mean he might have been a CIA man?'

'It's possible.'

'But that doesn't make sense,' Brady said. 'Surely your people are in cahoots with the CIA. I mean we're on the same side, aren't we?'

She gave a laugh, but she did not sound very amused. 'Oh, Steve my poor darling, sometimes you're so naîve it hurts, it really does.'

'Are you telling me there's no co-operation?'

'When it suits both partners perhaps, which is pretty rarely to say the least. More often there's about as much co-operation between us and them as there is between a mongoose and a cobra. We don't tell them our secrets and they don't tell us theirs. And they're so damned suspicious. They don't trust us, you see; they still remember Fuchs and Blake and Burgess and Maclean and Philby. They think we spend half our time leaking things to the Reds, and they look upon it as part of their divine duty to do their utmost to frustrate all such activities. It's a kind of occupational obsession with them. They're a pretty crazy bunch anyway.'

'For my money you're all crazy,' Brady said. But another unhappy thought had occurred to him: if Koulis had in fact been a CIA agent there were a lot of crazy bastards who were not going to like him very much if they ever found out what had happened to their man. He seemed to be losing all ways.

'I think you ought to try to get some sleep now,' Linda said. 'We've got a long day ahead of us.'

Sleep! She had to be joking.

★ ★ ★

They got away early in the morning. Wilkins ambled across as they were stowing the tent in the Volvo.

'Everything in order?'

'What do you think?' Brady said.

Wilkins appeared to be examining the ground beside the car, and Brady guessed that he was looking for any sign of blood. There were some oil patches but nothing else. Koulis had in fact bled very little.

'I think you'll manage,' Wilkins said.

'Without your help,' Linda told him, 'we could have been in real trouble. You've been very kind.'

Wilkins looked at her with a slight twist of the mouth that gave him a slightly cynical appearance. 'Kind! I wouldn't have called it that exactly. There are things one has to do.'

'You have a sense of duty?'

'You could call it that, I suppose. I may be seeing you again.'

'Do you think it likely?'

'More unlikely things have happened. You may need more help.'

'If we do, I hope you'll be on hand.'

'I'll try to be,' Wilkins said. 'I'll certainly try to be.'

Brady had spotted the blue Saab; it was parked unobtrusively behind a black Moskvich saloon. He wondered how long it would be before someone became curious about it and started looking for Mr. Koulis. But there was one consolation — if Linda's theory was correct Koulis had not been a KGB man. If he had been a CIA man it was bad enough, but it would have been a whole lot worse if he had been with the KGB because this was KGB country.

They reached Leningrad in less than two hours but stopped only for petrol, paying for it with some of the coupons they had bought at the Intourist office at the border.

'Don't we even get a look at the Winter Palace?' Brady asked.

'I thought you were the one who wanted to get the job finished,' she said. 'Maybe we'll do the sights on our way back.'

Brady shook his head. 'The only sight I want to see is the Finnish side of the frontier. And I won't be really happy until we're back in London.'

He drove very carefully, with Linda advising him and spotting the traffic signs. The last thing he wanted was to be involved in an accident or to contravene some minor point of law that would bring them to the attention of the police. But they cleared Leningrad without incident, and he changed places with the girl and let her drive for a while, because he was needing some sleep and it was not going to help matters if he dozed off at the wheel.

She was of the same opinion. 'You look like somebody with a bad hangover.'

'I've got plenty of reason for being badly hung over.'

'Well, there's one thing,' she said, giving him a critical inspection, 'that bruise on your jaw has just about gone.

Which is all to the good. We don't want people to think I've been knocking you about, do we?'

He noticed that she was even smiling. It was nice to know that someone could get a bit of amusement out of the situation; he doubted whether he could have found anything funny in it if he had searched with a magnifying glass.

Before he settled himself down in the seat he glanced back along the road. There was a heavy lorry coming up from the Leningrad direction and it went past the stationary Volvo with the diesel hammering and smoke coming out of the exhaust. There was nothing in sight behind the lorry.

'You're not still looking for that Saab, are you?' Linda said. 'You know what happened to the driver.'

'Yes, I know.' It must have been instinctive, that looking back, that fear of something on the tail; a sense of guilt. 'Mr. Koulis won't be driving it any more.'

When he woke up they were running smoothly along on a broad tarmac road and there were fields of corn on either side. His eyes were bleary and his mouth felt like the inside of a dried-out gum bottle. His head ached too and his limbs were stiff; one way and another, he was not exactly the old peak-of-fitness Steve Brady who had come out of Karsten's sauna a couple of days back. And that was a pity.

He sat up and licked his mouth with a scummy tongue, and Linda glanced at him briefly and then turned her attention back to the road.

'You've been snoring.'

'I never snore,' Brady said.

'There must be a ventriloquist in the back of the car then. Anyway, you were snoring like a pig.'

'Have you ever heard a pig snoring?'

'No.'

'Then how do you know I was snoring like one?'

'It was like a pig would snore.'

'I don't believe I was snoring.'

'You were,' she said.

It seemed hardly worth arguing about. Brady yawned. He reached out a hand

and switched on the car radio.

'You won't get anything out of that,' Linda said.

'Why not?'

'It's dead. I tried it.'

'What's wrong with it?'

'I expect it's the battery.'

'But it runs off the car battery, doesn't it?'

'No, it's not that type. It's got a dry battery.'

'How do you know?'

'Jaakko told me.'

'He might have seen to it that it was a new one then.'

'Maybe he didn't realise it was run down. Why do you want to listen to the radio anyway?'

'It would help to pass the time. Some of that grand old Russian music.'

'They may not be broadcasting any of that grand old Russian music. It may just be grand old Russian pep talks.'

Brady fiddled with the controls on the radio but it was no use; there was not a whisper coming out of the speaker. That battery had to be really dead — unless it was some other trouble.

'Why don't you leave it alone?' Linda said, and she sounded impatient, even a shade edgy. 'You aren't going to get anything out of it by playing around like that.'

'I could have a stab at fixing it.'

'With a dead battery?'

'Maybe we could buy a new one at the next town.'

'No,' she said sharply. 'You wouldn't get one of the right type.'

'We could try.'

'No,' she said again. 'Leave it alone, Steve, leave it alone.'

It struck him that she was getting a trifle heated over nothing more important than a radio battery, but he left it at that; he was not really bothered about it. But he did think that Karsten might have provided a set that worked; it showed a certain lack of consideration, even of efficiency; in neither of which departments would he have imagined the big Finn to have been at all deficient.

'Are you intending to reach Moscow tonight?' he asked.

She shook her head. 'It's too far. We should have to press it, and there's no point. We'll find another camping site and finish the journey in the morning.'

'As you please.' He would have been glad to get the business, whatever it might be, finished; but he knew that she was right; there was no sense in pushing things. He would feel all the better for a good night's sleep. Always supposing he managed to sleep.

★ ★ ★

The camping site was about two hundred kilometres on the Leningrad side of Moscow. Like the one they had camped at the previous night, it was in wooded surroundings with a lake nearby. Brady hoped there would be no need to dump a body in this particular lake; it was not something he wished to make a habit of doing.

'I just hope he was playing a lone hand, that's all.'

The girl looked at him inquiringly. 'What are you talking about?'

'Koulis.'

'Forget Koulis. He's not going to bother us any more.'

'I wish I could forget him, but a man you've killed has a way of sticking in your mind. Haven't you ever noticed that?'

'I've never killed anyone,' she said.

'No? Not even with that gun you handle so well?'

'Not with that gun. Not with anything.'

'Well, I'm glad to hear it,' he said. And he was. It was not the kind of thing he cared to imagine her doing, even in self-defence.

He managed to erect the tent without help from Wilkins. He had to, because Wilkins and his party had not put in an appearance; they were probably still hung up in Leningrad, doing the tour of that beautiful and historic city before moving on to Moscow for the Kremlin and Lenin's Tomb and Gum and all the rest of it. Linda gave him a hand, and they turned in early and, rather to his surprise, he slept soundly. The night was free from any alarms and excursions, and in the morning there was no blue Saab parked near the Volvo to make his heart skip a beat. They ate a good breakfast in the restaurant and Linda seemed in no hurry to get away.

'If we're in Moscow by the afternoon it will be early enough.'

'Early enough for what?'

'For what we have to do.'

Communicative as ever.

She walked over to the Volvo, and when he joined her he found her taking the battery out of the radio.

'I thought you weren't going to bother about that,' he said.

'Did you?'

It was a small flat-sided battery with two terminals on the top. It was not a make he had seen before and he supposed it was Finnish or possibly Swedish.

'Why have you taken it out?'

'Didn't you know,' she said, 'that you should never leave a dead battery in a radio? It can lead to corrosion.'

He would have laid a bet that she did not care two bent pins whether the radio got corroded or not, and when she put the battery in her handbag he was sure of it. But he made no further comment on the subject, having long since come to the conclusion that asking questions would get him nowhere; she told him just as much as she wished to tell and no more.

They left the camping site at about ten o'clock and drove without undue haste along the road to Moscow. They reached the outskirts of the capital early in the afternoon, and Brady noticed that the traffic was not nearly as dense as that of most West European cities, though there were rather more private cars than he had expected. No doubt as the Russians became more affluent the number would increase and they would come up against the same old problems of congestion and pollution that you found in London and Los Angeles, in Rome and Paris and Rio da Janeiro. Which was a happy prospect for Ivan Ivanovitch.

In the suburbs a lot of building appeared to be going on — large, multi-storey blocks of flats rising against the skyline.

'Homes for the happy workers,' Brady remarked.

'Presumably.'

'Do we have a home to go to?'

'The Yalta Hotel.'

'And you think we can find it?'

'We'll find it.'

She had a Moscow street map open on her knees, and when it came to reading a map Brady had to admit that she was pretty useful; on his own he would have been utterly lost. Eventually they got on to the Garden Ring and turned right, and a bit later they got off the Ring again and found the Yalta Hotel tucked away in a loop of the Moskva River.

The Yalta was not a modern hotel and the foyer was as old-fashioned as they came, but Brady had no time to think about the décor because the first person he saw when he and Linda walked in was Charles Wilkins sitting in a plush-covered armchair and reading a book.

Wilkins spotted them at once, and got up and came to meet them.

'This is indeed a pleasant surprise.'

'What are you doing here?' Brady

asked. 'I thought you'd still be in Leningrad.'

'Oh,' Wilkins said, 'I had some business in Moscow, so I came on ahead of my party.'

'Don't they need you?'

'They can get along very well without me. There's Simpson, you know; he's my deputy and he'll take charge.'

'So you had business in Moscow and it brought you to the Yalta Hotel?'

Wilkins grinned, showing his large teeth which gave him more than ever that look of a horse. 'Yes. A remarkable coincidence, don't you think?'

It was too remarkable. Brady refused to believe that it was a coincidence. Linda must surely have told him that they would be staying at the Yalta; her lack of any obvious surprise at finding him there pointed to the fact. Yet it seemed a trifle strange that she should have done so.

'So you're staying in this hotel too?'

'Yes, I often use it. It's quiet and convenient. As Russian hotels go, it's really not at all bad.' He turned to

183

Linda. 'Were you planning to go out this evening?'

This question, fired off so abruptly, struck Brady as rather strange too, and even slightly ill-mannered. But she appeared to accept it as perfectly natural and answered without hesitation.

'Yes, I had intended doing so.'

'And you can find your way?'

'I don't think there will be any difficulty in doing that.'

'Ah! Well, if you should need any help — '

'I'm sure it won't be necessary.'

'One hopes not. But things don't always go quite according to plan, do they? One meets unforeseen snags.' Brady got the impression that Wilkins was referring in an oblique sort of way to the unfortunate Mr. George Koulis, though he did not mention his name. 'If you do meet any snag, remember old Charles, eh?'

'And that we English always stick together?' Brady said.

Wilkins laughed. 'Precisely. Hit the nail exactly on the head, old man.'

'I'll remember,' Linda said.

They checked in at a desk presided over by a stout middle-aged female wearing gold-rimmed glasses. Apparently a room had been reserved for them, by whom Brady had no idea; perhaps Linda had arranged it through Intourist. The middle-aged female regarded them with a strictly neutral expression on her heavy features and addressed herself exclusively to Linda after discovering that Brady did not understand Russian. He had a feeling that she rather despised him for it.

The room was on the third floor and they went in a lift which matched the style of the foyer; it creaked and wheezed as it ascended, rather like an old man suffering from shortage of breath and arthritis in the joints. The room was clean but somewhat Spartan in its furnishing. Brady crossed to the window and he could see the river and a motor-barge chugging along, and away to the left a bridge.

He said: 'You told Wilkins we were coming here, of course.'

'Let's not talk about that,' she said quickly.

He detected a note of warning in her voice, and it occurred to him that perhaps she was afraid the room might be bugged. Perhaps all hotel rooms in Moscow were bugged.

'All right, if you don't want to.' He moved away from the window and caught her in his arms and kissed her. 'I love you, Mrs. Brady,' he said. If any bugs were picking that up they were welcome to it. 'Don't you think we ought to do something about it?'

'You're an idiot, Steve,' she said, and she began to laugh. He laughed too. It was good to have something to laugh about.

11

Between Friends

'I shall be going out this evening,' she said.

'That's what I thought,' Brady said.

They were having a meal in the dining-room of the Yalta Hotel. There was a good deal of noise in there — the clatter of dishes and cutlery, conversation, background music; he did not think there would be any bugging.

'You'd better stay here.'

'Now, that,' Brady said, 'doesn't seem at all a good plan. Not to me, it doesn't.'

'And why not, pray?'

'Linda, my sweet, you're not thinking very hard, and that's not like you. I ask you, is it the natural thing for a lovely young wife to go out on her own for the evening while her handsome young husband stays behind in the hotel? Come now, is it?'

She thought about it and had to admit that it was not really the natural thing.

'So don't you think I'd better come along too and help deliver that dud radio battery to whoever it is you've got to deliver it to?'

She gave him a sharp glance. 'Who said I was going to deliver a dud battery to anyone?'

'Nobody said so. I just worked it out for myself. Why, I asked myself, is she taking so much care of a worn-out battery? Why has she put it in her handbag so that she can carry it around with her? Is that, I asked myself, the kind of thing people usually do with old batteries? And the answer I came up with was: no, it certainly is not. And then I got it: there had to be something you were carrying into Russia and it was a thousand to one it was something hidden away in the Volvo; something you brought from London and passed to Jaakko to stow in the car that he was going to supply. I'd worked that much out already. What I hadn't worked out was where it was hidden; and it didn't even hit me when the radio failed to work and you gave me that stuff about Jaakko telling you it ran off a dry battery. Why would he bother to tell you that anyway? But when you took the battery out and shoved it in your handbag I knew it had to be that. And that's what Koulis was looking for, wasn't it?'

'You're the one who's doing the guessing.'

Things were beginning to fit into place in Brady's mind. 'And when he came out to the island that night he must have thought you still had it with you. But he would have been disappointed anyway, wouldn't he? Because you'd already given it to Jaakko to hide in the Volvo.'

She said nothing; just looked at him, waiting.

'But if Koulis was working for the CIA, why would he be trying to get hold of it? It doesn't make sense. So maybe he was a free-lance after all; maybe he just wanted to get his hands on it so that he could sell it to the highest bidder. Yes, that's it; maybe Koulis was working for nobody but himself.'

The possibility appealed to him; because if Koulis had been working on his own no one was likely to miss him and start looking round for the man who had taken his name off the register. If he could have been sure of that, it would have taken a lot of weight off his mind. But there was still another question: how did Koulis get to know what Linda was doing anyway? How did he know that something was being carried into Russia and that it might be worth his while to pick it up? Well, one thing was certain: he would not be answering that question for himself — not in this world.

'What is it, Linda?'

'What is what, Steve?'

'The battery of course.'

'Don't you think it's just a battery?'

'Ah, come off it,' Brady said. 'You know it's not just a battery.'

'Do I?'

'Sure, you do. So tell me. What is it?'

'I don't know.'

'You expect me to believe that?'

'I don't care whether you believe it or

not. It just happens to be the truth.'

It could be at that, he supposed. She was just a courier; no need for her to know what she was carrying; safer perhaps not to.

'Well, at least,' Brady said, 'you're not denying that you do have to deliver the battery to someone?'

'If it'll set your mind at rest, yes, I'll admit that is what I do have to do.'

'It doesn't set my mind at rest in the slightest, but I'm glad you've decided to come clean at last. There should always be mutual trust between a man and his wife.'

'Is that so?'

'You bet it's so. And now you're going to take me along when you go on your little errand, aren't you?'

'You may not enjoy it.'

'I'm not expecting to, but it'll be a lot more enjoyable than sitting by myself in this damned hotel wondering what the devil is happening to you.'

'Nothing's going to happen to me.'

'I hope not. Because if it happens to you it looks like happening to me too.

I suppose you know where to find your contact?'

'Of course I know where to find him. Do you take me for an absolute fool?'

'Linda, my darling,' Brady said, 'I don't know what I take you for, I really don't. So let's just say I take you.'

★ ★ ★

They got on to the Metro at one of those early ornate stations that had been built in Krushchev's time. It put Brady in mind of a Victorian public bath, all marble and glazed tile, and the only thing missing was a fountain bubbling from the mouth of a petrified fish. He was pretty much on edge again and there seemed to be a lot of square, hard-faced men standing around, any of whom might have been members of the KGB. Brady tried to assume an air of innocence, which is not one of the easiest things to do when feeling as guilty as a burglar caught with his hand in the safe. That he was not making a very successful job of it was evident from the reaction of his companion.

'Do you,' she said, 'have to look quite so hangdog?'

'I was trying to look innocent.'

'Well, you don't. You look like a petty thief.'

'I feel like a petty thief. And I think we're being followed.'

'Oh, God,' she said, 'not that again. You always think we're being followed.'

'Sometimes I'm right.'

It was a statement she could not dispute, but at that moment the train arrived and they got in. They travelled quite some distance through parts of Moscow that Napoleon never saw, and Brady tried without any noticeable success to read the names of the stations as they came to them. It was typical Russian obscurantism, he reflected, to use 'C' for 'S' and turn the 'N's' the wrong way round, and he could only admire Linda's devotion to duty in mastering such a fiendish language.

They got out at one of the newer stations which had been constructed on more severely modern lines. The pillars were still apparently being made of marble, but they were rectangular in section and there were no ornamented curves to the roof. It was cleaner than a London tube station.

They came to the surface in the middle of what appeared to be a construction site; at least, there seemed to be a lot of building going on, and Brady came to the conclusion that Moscow must be having a housing drive.

'Where now?'

Linda consulted her street-map, frowning slightly, and he thought maybe she had lost the way, but finally she said: 'We take a bus from here. It's not very far.'

It was a warm evening and the bus was almost full. Brady spent the journey trying to recognise among the passengers any of the square, hard-faced men who had joined the Metro train with him and the girl. He found it difficult to be certain because, if Russians did not, as Chinese did, look all alike, to him a lot of them certainly did, and it was a likeness he did not much care for either.

The bus stopped.

'This is where we get off,' Linda said.

It was obviously one of the older parts of Moscow. A lot of the buildings had the grim, featureless look of prison blocks, and a few trees here and there seemed to be fighting a desperate rearguard action against the invading concrete. Again Linda was forced to consult her map, and as she was doing so a man came up and spoke to her. He was wearing a rather baggy blue suit and an open-necked cotton shirt, like a Londoner on a day-trip to Southend in the days before the affluent society came along to change all that and send the British working man off with his wife on the package flight to Majorca and the Costa Brava.

Brady felt himself getting that hangdog look again, and he would not have been surprised if the man had started calling up reinforcements. But nothing of that kind happened; Linda was talking to him with every sign of amicability, and then the man began pointing, and Linda nodded and smiled and seemed to be thanking him.

Then she turned to Brady. 'Come on,' she said, and started walking again.

The man said something to Brady too, but the only word of Russian he could remember offhand was that old favourite of Comrade Molotoff, 'Niet', and somehow he doubted whether that would fit the occasion. So he just gave the man one of the Brady grins and followed the girl.

'What did he want?'

'He wanted to direct us,' she said. 'He was very obliging.'

'He nearly gave me heart failure when he spoke to you.'

'You must have a weak heart.'

'It was strong enough before I got mixed up with you.'

'Oh, for goodness' sake, Steve,' she said, 'why do you have to moan so much? Anyone would think you weren't enjoying your holiday.'

'Well now,' Brady said, 'when it comes to that I suppose you could say it's like the curate's egg, good in parts. But unfortunately there are an awful lot of bad parts too, and I have a nasty feeling we may be getting close to one of them now.'

She gave him one of those contemptuous looks which seemed to say she had known jellyfish with stiffer back-bones, and walked on. They turned a corner and found themselves in a quiet street with a corrugated-iron fence on one side, behind which some demolition work had been going on, and some of the gaol-like concrete buildings on the other. There were a lot of cracks in the concrete, as though it had not been of very good quality or the foundations had settled, or both; and Brady guessed that the buildings had probably been erected in the twenties or thirties in the early days of the Communist regime. Time had not dealt kindly with them, but even at that they had lasted a good deal longer than most of the men who had helped to lay the foundations of the Party: some of them had had a very rapid decay.

Linda had stopped to read the numbers

at the entrance to one of the blocks when the car went past. It was a big black saloon, and it was noticeable because there were no other cars in the street. It went past slowly, and Brady could see three men sitting in it, and they were all wearing brown suits and felt hats with rather wide brims, as though they got their clothes at the same outfitter's. None of the men gave as much as a glance at Brady or the girl; they just stared straight ahead, and the car went on and turned the corner at the end of the street and disappeared.

'This is the place,' Linda said.

Brady was thinking about the car. 'Did you see that?'

'Did I see what?"

'That car with three men in it.'

'Yes, I saw it,' she said. 'So what?'

'I didn't like the look of it.'

'Is there anything in Moscow you do like the look of?'

'Well, did you like the look of it?'

'I didn't even think about it.'

'Don't you think you should? If you ask me, it was damned suspicious.'

'Now what,' she said, and she sounded exasperated, 'was suspicious about a car with three men in it?'

'Do you see any other cars around?'

'No. But private cars are not terribly thick on the ground, especially in this part of Moscow.'

'That's what I mean. So why did that one happen to go past just at this particular moment?'

'I suppose you're going to say you think it was following us?'

'I think it could have been.'

'All the way from the hotel? On the Metro?'

'It didn't have to follow us all the way. It could have been waiting at the Metro station where we got off.'

'Why would it be doing that? Nobody knew we were going to get off there.'

He saw that what she said was logical and that he was probably making something out of nothing. 'All right,' he said. 'Maybe they were just taking an evening ride; maybe they were going to a chess game or a vodka party.' But he was still not really happy about it. He was not happy about anything.

The door was open and they walked into a bare lobby smelling faintly of disinfectant and with corridors branching off to left and right. The lobby was deserted and there was a concrete stairway rising out of it, and that was bare and deserted also.

'It's on the second floor,' Linda said.

They began to climb, the tread of their feet on the concrete steps making a hollow sound that echoed back from the walls. A lot of feet had trodden those same steps in the course of the years and had worn them down until their edges were no longer straight but gently curving. When they reached the first landing a man and a woman passed them on the way down, talking animatedly and showing no interest in anything but their own conversation. On the second floor were two more corridors leading away to left and right, and there were numbered doors opening off the corridors. Linda studied the numbers and began to walk down the corridor on the right, finally coming to a halt at a door with the number '36' painted on it. There was a bell-push at the side of the door. She pressed it, but there was no anwering sound of a bell or a buzzer.

'It doesn't work,' Brady said. He felt a strong urge to go away then, using the failure of the bell as an excuse; but the decision was not his to make.

Linda abandoned the bell-push and rapped on the door with her knuckles. They waited, listening. There was no sound from inside.

'Nobody at home,' Brady said. 'Let's go.'

'Wait,' Linda said. She rapped on the door again, rather more loudly. Still there was no response from within.

'It's no good,' Brady said. 'We may as well go.'

'No.'

She turned the door-knob and pushed. Creaking slightly, the door opened.

'You can't do that,' Brady protested. 'You can't just walk into somebody's private apartment. It's not legal. It's — '

But she was already doing it, and after one swift guilt-ridden glance to left and right to make sure there was no one in the corridor to see him, he followed her in.

'Better shut the door,' she said.

Brady shut the door.

It was not a large room and it was not very well furnished. There was a window on the far side; the window was open but it was still warm and close in the room. There was a table pushed up against one wall and there were a few chairs that were in rather worse condition than those in Brady's own rooms in London. There were books everywhere — on the table, on a kind of side-board where they were mixed up with bottles and plates and tumblers, and piled in heaps on the floor. Notebooks and manuscripts, too, were scattered about in haphazard fashion with no apparent concern for order; it was all chaotic and untidy, as though nothing was ever cleared up or stowed away.

Brady became aware of a faint sound like a low murmur that rose and fell with monotonous regularity. It puzzled him, but Linda crossed to the right hand side of the room, drew back a curtain and revealed a kind of alcove in which was an iron bed. Lying on the bed and snoring lightly was a man wearing a short-sleeved shirt and a pair of denim trousers. His feet were bare and he had a mop of dark, curly hair and a wispy beard.

Linda walked straight up to the bed, gripped the man's shoulder and shook him. To Brady it seemed to be taking one hell of a liberty to walk into a man's room without a word of invitation while he was snatching a bit of sleep and start mauling his shoulder; it was an invasion of privacy, it was against all the tenets of good manners, and it was probably breaking the law.

'You can't do that,' he said again.

But again she had done it, and the man was awake. She stepped back a pace or two, and the man swung his legs over the edge of the bed and just sat there staring at her, as though not sure whether she was real or whether he was still dreaming and she was part of the dream.

She gave him about ten seconds to

collect his wits, and then, speaking in very slow, deliberate English, she said:

'It is a long way to Vladivostock on the Trans-Siberian Railway.'

Brady's immediate thought was that everything had been a bit too much for her and that she had gone quietly barmy; and he would have said that the man on the bed was thinking much the same thing, only in Russian. But then the man pushed his fingers through his hair, puckered up his eyes as though putting the screws on his memory, and answered, also in English:

'That is so. But what is a journey between friends when the rolling-stock is in good condition?'

12

Vladimir

So they still did it, they really did. He would not have believed it if he had not heard it. It made him laugh. Who the devil had dreamed up those two observations? Stewart Cobb? Yes, it had to be Cobb. Funny man, Cobb, in his way.

Linda and the man, who was still sitting on the bed, did not join in the laughter; they looked at him and they were not even smiling. He stopped laughing; it was not funny really. He supposed they had to have these methods of proving their identity; in the old days kings' messengers had carried royal rings, but these were modern times. All the same, he had not imagined it would be done like that. But it had been, and it was okay; at least they had come to the right place, had found the right man; that was something.

Linda turned again to the man: 'Vladimir?'

The man nodded. He stood up. He was not much taller than the girl and he had an undernourished appearance. He looked to be about thirty-five or so and his face had a yellowy tinge. He was nervous too; he could not keep his hands still and there was a tick under his left eye.

Linda backed out of the alcove and he followed her. He made a kind of half-gesture towards one of the chairs, but it was not really an invitation and it just faded out. He seemed not to know what to do with his feet, and he kept combing his tangled hair with his fingers. Brady began to feel sorry for him; he was the kind of person who excited pity; he looked so helpless. It was difficult to understand how such a man came to be a secret agent; but perhaps this was his camouflage, a mask assumed in order to avert suspicion.

'You were expecting a visit?' Linda asked.

Again he passed his fingers through his

hair with that bemused expression on his face. 'Visit?'

'You were expecting me? Someone. A courier.'

'No. No one.'

She looked surprised. 'You were not warned?'

'No.'

It was obvious that there had been some slip-up, a failure in the lines of communication. Brady wondered what she would do now. He supposed her orders had simply been to deliver the battery to Vladimir; but if Vladimir had no knowledge of the business did the order still hold good? He could see the frown on her face as she tried to work that one out, but he did not interfere; it was not his department.

Finally she seemed to come to a decision. She opened her handbag, pulled out the battery and stood it on the table.

'I was instructed to deliver this to you.'

Vladimir walked across the room and stared at the battery. Then he looked at the girl with bewilderment in his eyes.

'I do not understand.'

It was a plain statement of fact; he was not fooling. He just did not understand. Brady had a sudden feeling of the ground shifting under his feet. Something was wrong, and where did they go from here?

The girl was uncertain too. Until this moment she had known precisely what to do; she had been acting according to the instructions received in London. But now this complication had cropped up and apparently there were no contingency plans designed to cover it.

'You do not know what this is?'

'It is a battery,' Vladimir said.

'No, it is not a battery.'

Vladimir looked even more confused. He glanced at Brady as if seeking help in that quarter. Brady could give him none.

'Not a battery?'

'No.'

'Then what is it?'

'I don't know. I thought you would know.'

'No,' Vladimir said.

It could have gone on like that for a long time, getting nowhere, if there had not been an interruption. But suddenly the door opened and two men walked in. Brady knew then that he had been right about the black saloon, because the men were wearing brown suits and felt hats, and it was a thousand to one that they were two of the three who had been in the car.

One of them took a few steps to the left as if to avoid blocking his companion's line of sight, while the other closed the door behind him and stood with his back against it. It was a very broad back, and so was the other man's, but what gave things a really unpleasant aspect was the fact that both men were carrying pistols. Moreover, they had that kind of hard, uncompromising look which said that they were prepared to use the weapons without any hesitation if the need should arise. Brady very much hoped that the need would not arise, and he for one meant to do nothing whatever that would give anyone a reason for feeling that the need had arisen. Like rushing at the men, for example, or trying to knock the guns out of their hands or making an attempt to escape by the window. Seeing that it was a second-floor window, escape by that route would hardly have been a practical proposition anyway, quite apart from the likelihood of getting a bullet between the shoulder-blades for his pains.

'Don't do anything heroic, Steve,' Linda said warningly.

'I'm not likely to,' he said. 'You know me.'

He doubted whether Vladimir was likely to either; he looked petrified with fright, and again it occurred to Brady that he must be a very tenth-rate agent and not the sort who would be resourceful enough to deal effectively with a couple of obviously tough KGB men. And when you came to think about it, it would have taken the deuce of a lot of resourcefulness to do that anyway.

The man who was not standing by the door said something in Russian and made a gesture with his pistol. He had a hand like a slab of raw meat wrapped round the butt of the gun and a thick finger on the trigger.

'He says we're to get back against the wall,' Linda said.

'Well, let's do that,' Brady said; and he saw that Vladimir had already done so. Vladimir seemed to know what was good for his health.

They backed up against the wall, not once taking their eyes off the KGB men, and then the one who was dishing out the orders opened his mouth again and let some more words leak out of the gap.

'He says we're to put our hands on our heads,' Linda said.

They did that too.

The talking man left it to the one by the door to watch them while he walked over to the table and examined the radio battery. Brady could tell from the way he looked at it that he knew very well it was not just a battery. He picked it up and seemed to weigh it in his hand, and then he slipped it into the pocket of his jacket, where it produced a bulge that would have made a tailor's heart bleed.

After that the man looked at Brady and the girl and Vladimir, still backed up against the wall with their hands on their heads, and Brady could almost see his mind working on the question of what to do with them. If Brady had had a working knowledge of the Russian language he would have told the man not to worry, because he and the girl, if not Vladimir, were not going to make any trouble; they were going to get out of Russia just as fast as it was possible to do so, and he for one was never coming back. It was the first time he had regretted his ignorance of the language, but it was a bit late to start thinking about the kind of crash course that Linda had taken because time seemed to be running out.

The man still had the pistol gripped in that slab of raw meat he called his hand, and he was moving it about in a pretty alarming fashion; but suddenly he gave a laugh and said something to the other man, who reached out with his left hand and pulled the door open; and Brady thought: My god, they're going; they're leaving us in one piece; they've got what they want and they're not bothering about anything else. Halleluiah!

He felt like giving three cheers for Mother Russia and hugging somebody, which would have been difficult with his hands still on his head. But then Wilkins came in and things started getting complicated again.

Wilkins came in so fast he might have been a sprinter getting off the starting-blocks. He came in and kicked the door shut with his heel, and he was carrying a small gun in his right hand. It was so small that it made very little noise, just a cracking sound like the snapping of a twig; but it was enough to stop the man by the door in his tracks, and when the other man, the one who had laughed, started having ideas about using his own gun — but not having them quickly enough — it stopped him too.

'You can take your hands off your head now, old man,' Wilkins said. 'It looks a bit silly.'

Brady had forgotten about his hands. He let them fall to his sides. Wilkins put the gun away in his pocket. The two KGB men were not moving. Brady decided that Wilkins must have had a lot of practice with a pistol, but he was not sure that he felt very happy about it.

'You've done it now,' he said. 'You really have.'

'It was necessary,' Wilkins said; and he was as calm as a surgeon who has just removed a malignant growth.

'It wasn't necessary. They were going.'

Wilkins smiled. 'Perhaps. But not empty-handed, I imagine.' He turned to the girl. 'You'd better take it back. It's obvious there's been some awful balls-up somewhere.'

She crossed over to where the KGB man was lying and took the battery from his pocket. He was making no objection, but Brady thought she seemed glad to get away from him again. She was looking sick. She put the battery in her handbag.

'Vladimir has no idea what it is,' she said.

Wilkins nodded. 'Somebody's been dealing from the bottom of the pack.' He gave a swift, all-embracing glance round the room, as though imprinting everything on his memory, and it almost seemed that his nose twitched slightly with disdain. 'Well, we'd better be going.'

'What about him?' Brady said, nodding towards Vladimir, who had slumped into one of the dilapidated armchairs and had buried his face in his hands, the picture of utter despair.

'Well?' Wilkins said. 'What about him?'

'We can't just leave him here with these.' Brady indicated the dead KGB men.

'We can't carry them away.'

'We could take him with us.'

'No,' Wilkins said. 'That's out of the question. It's going to be difficult enough as it is.'

'So you'll just abandon him?'

'He hasn't been much help, has he?'

Brady stared at Wilkins. Wilkins's long, bony face revealed no trace of emotion.

'You're a hard bastard,' Brady said.

'In this kind of job you have to be.'

Brady turned to Linda. 'Do you think

we should leave him to sort this mess out?'

There was a hunted look in her eyes. She glanced at Vladimir's hunched figure, then back at Brady. 'There's nothing else we can do.' She seemed to be pleading with him to understand.

'We could take him with us,' Brady said again.

'It's not possible, Steve. Don't you see it's not.'

'No,' he said, 'I don't see it.'

Vladimir raised his head then and spoke for the first time since the KGB men had walked into the room. 'I do not wish to go with you. What use would it be?' He looked at the bodies and his face was haggard. 'I am finished, finished.'

Wilkins had his hand on the door. 'Come along. There's no time to waste. The third man may be coming up to see what's holding these two if we don't hurry.'

Brady had forgotten about the driver. Now he saw a snag. 'Where is he?'

'He's sitting in the car outside the street door.'

'That's torn it,' Brady said. 'He knows us. He had a look at us before we came up.'

'I'll deal with him,' Wilkins said. 'Now move.'

He opened the door. Linda walked out into the corridor. Brady gave a last glance at Vladimir, who shook his head sadly, as much as to say that there was nothing to be done about it, then turned and followed the girl. Wilkins closed the door.

There was no one in the lobby at the bottom of the stairs. They could see the black saloon parked outside.

'Wait here,' Wilkins said.

He walked out of the building and straight up to the car. He had his back towards them but they could see that he was leaning in through the car window, apparently talking to the driver. A few seconds later he turned and came back to the doorway.

'Come,' he said.

Brady hesitated and Wilkins snapped at him impatiently: 'Come. It's all right.'

As they passed the car Brady noticed

that the driver appeared to be asleep. He wondered how Wilkins had done it; he had certainly not used the gun. A swift prick with a hypodermic perhaps? What did it matter? The thing was done.

★ ★ ★

The Land-Rover was parked three blocks away. They were clear of Moscow by the time the shadows had begun to close in. Linda had suggested going back to the Yalta Hotel for their luggage and the Volvo, but Wilkins had firmly vetoed that idea.

'The hotel may be watched, and it would use up too much time which we can't afford to lose. The object now is to get you out of the country as quickly as possible.'

Brady, riding in the back of the Land-Rover, was all in favour of that. But he still did not quite get Wilkins: this was the second time the man had stepped in at a critical moment and had proceeded to take charge.

'How the devil did you happen to be on hand?'

Wilkins grinned, with an oddly savage twist to his mouth. 'I thought you might need some help.'

'You knew we were going to see Vladimir?'

'I knew your charming wife had to make a delivery to him. I decided to get there first and keep an eye on things. I saw the other boys arrive.'

'How do you come to know so much?'

'It's my job, old man. Orders from London were to watch over you two lovebirds like a fairy godmother.'

'So you're in the same business?'

'Don't tell me you hadn't guessed,' Wilkins said. 'You're not as thick as that.'

'It did cross my mind,' Brady admitted. 'So you had orders from Cobb?'

Wilkins shook his head. 'No, not Cobb.'

So there were other fingers in the pie. Just how many? Brady wondered. And just how much did one finger know of what another finger was doing? But he did not pursue that line of inquiry. He doubted whether Wilkins would have revealed much anyway.

'I take it then that our meeting at the border was not entirely accidental.'

'Well, yes, actually it was. I couldn't plan to that degree of accuracy. I was hoping to pick you up at the first camping site, but the border contact was a lucky bonus; it simplified matters.'

'And you really do the other job?'

'It's my cover, old man.'

'You're neglecting it. Maybe you'll get the push.'

'If nothing worse than that happens,' Wilkins said, 'I'll be happy. What I'd like to know is how the KGB boys got on to you so smartly. I don't much care for that.'

'I'd like to know too,' Linda said. 'And I'd like to know why Vladimir hadn't been put in the picture.'

Brady began thinking about Vladimir again. They had certainly cooked his goose; they had left him up to the neck in trouble, and he was not the type of man who was likely to be able to cope with that kind of trouble. So what would he do?

He put the question to Wilkins.

'Damned if I know,' Wilkins said. 'I'm not a ruddy crystal-gazer.'

'Do you think he'll kill himself?'

'Oh, no.' Linda said quickly. 'He wouldn't do that.' But Brady knew by the way she said it that she thought he might.

'I'm not so sure,' Wilkins said. 'We left some guns lying around. It would be the easy way out. And from our point of view it might be for the best.'

'How do you mean?' Brady asked.

'I should have thought that was obvious. If he stays alive he's bound to talk. With two dead KGB men in his room and another in the car outside, what kind of a story could he come up with to clear himself? They'll get the truth out of him, you can be sure of that. So we'd better hope he does kill himself. Perhaps I should have done the job for him.'

Wilkins was not fooling, Brady was sure of that; he really was regretting that he had not made certain of Vladimir's silence while he had had the chance. Wilkins was certainly a hard bastard and no mistake.

'What does Vladimir do?' Brady asked.

'Do?'

'For a living. Apart from working for your people.'

'He's a writer,' Wilkins said. 'Technical stuff. He's got some useful contacts. Correction — had some useful contacts; they'll be no more good to us now. Frankly I'd never have touched him in the first place. You can't trust bloody writers.'

It was still not dark when they got on to the Leningrad road. Wilkins was soon giving the Land-Rover a lot of stick and it was pretty bumpy in the back. Brady wondered whether the intention was to go straight for the border and hope to get through before the alarm was sounded, but he did not ask; he simply came to the conclusion in his own mind that the chances of doing that were about as slim as a spider's thread. The way Wilkins was pushing the Land-Rover along, too, they could soon be in other trouble — like a collision with one of those heavy lorries for instance. That would surely dish things.

But Wilkins was a good driver, and when it got really dark he eased down slightly on the speed and it was more comfortable in the back.

Brady was feeling some regret for the luggage abandoned at the Yalta Hotel. He was not in sufficiently affluent circumstances to be able to write off that amount of clothing without a pang; some of it had been nearly new, bought with the advance that Cobb had dished out under pressure. He wondered whether he could sting Cobb for replacements, because he was dead certain it was going to be no use writing to the Yalta Hotel when he got back to England and asking them to send the stuff on, carriage paid. Always supposing he got back to England. Which seemed none too certain at the moment. And even less so when they came to the road-block.

13

Road-block

'Hell!' Wilkins said. 'Bloody flaming hell and damnation!'

He took his foot off the accelerator and started to apply the brakes, and the Land-Rover slowed to a walking pace as they moved up to the road-block and finally came to a halt.

'What's going on?' Brady asked. 'What is it?'

Wilkins gave a hard sort of laugh, more like a bark than anything else. 'Trouble, that's what it is, old man; trouble. Damned if I thought they'd have worked so fast. This really bitches things.'

They had made a good job of it. Brady could not help reflecting that when the Russians set up a road-block they really set one up and no half-measures. There was a big articulated lorry slewed across the road, and there was no way round the tail unless you had a tank and were prepared to mow down a few trees. At the front end, where it might have been possible to get by, there was a black saloon car parked so as to make a chicane, and that was that. Check! And maybe even checkmate!

Wilkins had twitched off the headlights, but the Russians had fixed up a floodlight of some kind and Brady could see several men in uniforms who looked like police and probably were. Two of them strolled towards the Land-Rover, not hurrying. They had no need to hurry; nobody was running away. On the road somewhere between Moscow and Leningrad, where would you go?

One of the policemen came up to the window on Wilkins's side and said something to him. Wilkins answered. The other policeman went round to the opposite side and spoke to the girl. Brady would have liked to know what was being said, but he felt that it was hardly the time to break in with a request for a translation.

Wilkins began feeling in an inside pocket. He pulled out his passport and handed it to the first policeman. Linda took her passport out of her handbag and gave it to the second policeman. Brady decided to get in on the act and he fished out his passport too. Wilkins relayed it on to the first policeman, who examined it carefully and then put his head into the Land-Rover and gave Brady a thorough examination too. Brady felt that hangdog look taking over again and the butterflies ganging up in his stomach.

The policeman had one of those faces that look as though they have been hacked out of a block of concrete with a blunt chisel and a couple of stones plugged in for eyes — disbelieving eyes. He was not young and it was possible that he had an aching tooth or sore feet or a filthy liver, because it was obvious that something was making him gloomy. The other policeman was younger and looked more cheerful, but he had only Linda Manning to deal with, so perhaps he had more to be cheerful about.

Brady was waiting for the older

policeman to tell them to get out of the Land-Rover, but he seemed to be taking a long time to make up his mind about it. He started talking to Wilkins again, and it was not necessary to know the language to realise that there was some interrogation going on. Brady just hoped Wilkins had a good story, but he would not have laid a bent copeck on the chances of any kind of story getting them out of the spot they were in at that moment.

The interrogation seemed to go on for a long time, and the butterflies kept fluttering around inside and he was thinking of three dead KGB men back in Moscow, and maybe a dead writer as well. Or a live writer singing away like a lark and telling all he knew. And he wondered what in hell had ever induced him to take on a job like this. But he knew the answer to that one: two hundred pounds and Linda Manning, that was what. He must have been crazy.

He heard a kind of rumbling sound behind, and when he looked back he saw that another heavy lorry had crept up on their tail, and now they were properly wedged in. It made no real difference to the situation because there had never been any chance of wriggling out of the trap anyway, but it made things seem worse, and heaven knew they had seemed bad enough before.

And then suddenly the policeman with the concrete face stopped asking questions, handed the passports back, and stepped away from the Land-Rover. He gave a signal with his hand, and Wilkins restarted the engine and got the vehicle moving. He took it very carefully round the back of the big saloon and then round the front of the articulated lorry; and Brady saw that the cab had taken a bit of a beating, as though some ill-natured person had been at work on it with a sledge-hammer. But that was nothing to what had happened to the smaller lorry on the other side, which until then they had been unable to see: this had really suffered, and as the Land-Rover went past a body was just being extracted from the wreckage.

'What happened?' Brady asked. 'For

God's sake, what happened?'

'You can see for yourself.' Wilkins sounded edgy now that the immediate crisis was past. 'It was an accident, just an accident.'

'You mean they weren't looking for us?'

'No.'

'Then why did it take them so long to let us through?'

'They don't like tourists to drive around at night. They say it's for the good of the tourists — in case they break down miles from a service station — but that's all eyewash if you ask me; it's because they're so damned suspicious. That policeman wanted to know where we'd come from and where we were going. I said we were staying at a camping site a few kilometres further on, that we'd been to Moscow and were late starting back.'

'Do you think he'll check up with the camping site?'

'It's possible. On the other hand he may let it slide. They seem to have got quite a job on their plates at the moment without worrying about us.'

Brady hoped Wilkins was right about that, but he was not very confident of it. It was sheer bad luck running into an accident like that; and now the police had their names and it might not be long before they were linked up with the Moscow business. Hell!

Wilkins was pushing the Land-Rover along again as though he knew that time might be running out. Brady caught the sense of urgency, and he was still feeling like a bundle of chewed-up nerves and sick in the stomach with a headache thrown in for good measure, and he wondered how Linda could be so calm. She ought to have been having hysterics or going into a dead faint or something. But of course girls had given up hysterics and fainting about the time when they got the vote, and nowadays they were as tough as men, and maybe tougher.

'Where exactly are we going?' he asked.

'You'll see,' Wilkins said.

'That's what I like about you people,' Brady told him. 'You're so informative.'

Wilkins just grunted.

It was about three hours later when they arrived. They had passed through a small town and come out on the Leningrad side when Wilkins suddenly slowed down, turned off the main road, drove on a short distance, made one or two more acute turns, and finally came to a halt.

'This is where you get out,' he said.

They got out. There was a certain amount of sickly grey light, indicating that dawn might not be far away, and the air was chilly. Brady could see the dark outline of some buildings but no sign of life.

'Wait here,' Wilkins said. 'I'll be back in a minute.'

He walked away and disappeared in the gloom. Linda was standing by the bonnet of the Land-Rover and Brady moved closer to her for company.

'Do you think he knows what he's doing?'

'I think he knows,' she said. 'But whether or not it's the right thing is another matter.'

That was just what he needed

— something to cheer him up. But maybe she was not feeling so cheerful herself; maybe she too could have done with a bit of cheering up; maybe she was not really so tough. He would have said something cheering if he could have thought of anything, but he was clean out of ideas in that line. He was still trying to think of something when Wilkins came back.

'All right,' Wilkins said. 'Come with me.'

They went with him, and a few seconds later they found themselves in a room that was practically bare except for a plain wooden table, a couple of rough settles and some bunk beds against one wall. It looked like a kind of doss-house or barrack-room, and there was a lingering odour of stale sweat and stale tobacco smoke and stale food; but nobody was using it just then.

There was one other person there, and he looked as though he had been roused from sleep and had just thrown on a few clothes in a great hurry. He was fat and his hair was tousled and he was unshaven, and now and then he yawned, revealing a lot of teeth that could have used some attention from a dentist.

'This is Yuri,' Wilkins said. 'He will look after you until I get back. Don't tell him anything.'

'You're going somewhere?' Brady said.

'I have to make arrangements. If you're hungry Yuri will get you some food. You can pay him if you wish.'

'How long shall we be here?' the girl asked.

'Today. Don't wander off. Better try to get some sleep.'

Brady did not care for the sound of it, but they were in Wilkins's hands and had to trust him. He was not at all sure that he trusted Yuri, but apparently Wilkins did — within limits. To Brady the Russian looked about as trustworthy as a starving hyena, but that might have been to misjudge him on the evidence of his appearance, which could have been an unreliable guide to his character.

Wilkins went away and they heard the Land-Rover start up, and then the sound of it moving off, fading into silence. Brady had a feeling of having been abandoned, but that was nonsense; Wilkins would be back. Unless he got into a tangle with the police or the KGB. Pleasant thought.

He looked at the girl. 'What do we do if he doesn't come back?'

'Why shouldn't he come back?'

'I could think of a dozen reasons.'

'He'll be back,' she said; but he doubted whether she was as confident as she would have had him believe. And she must have known as well as he did that if Wilkins did not come back, for whatever reason, they were well and truly in the soup.

Yuri was staring at them, his head a little on one side, his eyes swivelling from one to the other and a kind of half-grin twisting his blubbery lips. Brady guessed that he did not understand English and was perhaps curious as to what they were saying.

'Are you hungry?' Linda asked.

'I can wait for breakfast,' Brady said, 'but there's something that won't wait till then. Would you mind asking him where the john is?'

She asked him, and Yuri showed the way. It was at the end of a dark passage and it smelt of strong disinfectant. There were probably other smells but the disinfectant overpowered them. It was a very primitive john, but Brady was not fussy about a thing like that; it served its purpose. When he returned he found the girl alone.

'Are you going to take Charles's advice?'

'What advice?' she asked.

'To get some sleep.'

She walked over to the bunks. They were equipped with mattresses and rough grey blankets, but no sheets. The blankets were dirty and she seemed to be repelled by them.

'It's certainly not the Savoy,' Brady said. 'Come to that, it's not even the Yalta, but you can have a bath later. At least, I hope you can.' He thought of Jaakko Karsten's island retreat with its sauna, and it seemed pretty desirable just then; desirable and a hell of a long way off. 'Come, it's nearly daylight and we may be in for another sleepless night. Better get some rest while you can.'

She saw the sense of that, and finally kicked off her shoes and climbed on to one of the bunks. Brady noticed that she kept her handbag with her, the strap twisted round her wrist. With the battery inside it, she was not likely to let it out of her sight if she could help it.

He put the light out and crawled into one of the other bunks. It had that sour, sweaty smell about it, but he was really tired and getting to sleep was no trouble at all.

* * *

It was broad daylight when he awoke. Linda was leaning over the bunk and shaking him. He felt filthy and unshaven, and the gum had got in his mouth again. His first thought was that something had gone wrong and that they had to get out of there fast.

'Is it the police?' he said; and he already had one leg over the side and was

236

prepared to make a bolt for it, though he had no idea where to go.

But she stopped him. 'No, it isn't the police. It's breakfast.'

And then he smelt the food and saw that Yuri was putting some dishes on the table, and he realised just how hungry he was. He looked at his wrist-watch; it was nearly ten o'clock.

'It's a late breakfast,' he said.

'Yuri thought we needed a good sleep.'

'Very considerate of him.'

The Russian glanced at him and grinned. Brady decided that he looked very little more prepossessing in daylight, but maybe Yuri was thinking the same about him. He got off the bunk and pulled his shoes on.

'Wilkins hasn't come back?'

'Not yet.'

'I wonder where he's gone.'

'He said he was going to make arrangements.'

'Yes, that's what he said.'

'Don't you think it was the truth?'

'I don't know what to think.'

'Don't you trust him?'

'I haven't been acquainted with him very long, so I don't know much about him.'

'He's done a lot for you in a short time.'

'Yes,' Brady said; and he was thinking about what Wilkins had done — like killing three KGB men. 'He has, hasn't he?'

'Just be patient, Steve,' she said. 'And relax.'

He seemed to have heard that one before.

It was a good solid breakfast, but Brady noticed that Linda appeared to have little appetite, merely toying with the food.

'Are you feeling all right?' he asked.

She answered a little edgily: 'Of course I am. Why shouldn't I be?'

'You're not eating much.'

'I never eat much breakfast.'

He knew that that was not true; he had seen her tucking into the first meal of the day on other occasions with no apparent concern for the calorie intake. So maybe it was worry that was putting her off the food; maybe under that calm, unruffled exterior she was as worried as he was. She would have been scarcely human if she had not been; there was a devil of a lot to be worried about.

When Yuri came back for the dishes Brady gave him some roubles. He looked happy, so there must have been enough. Quite possibly there were too many, but what did it matter? It was public money.

The morning passed away slowly. They stayed in the room. There was one dirty window, and through it a kind of yard was visible and some dilapidated out-houses.

'What is this place?' Brady asked.

'You know as much about is as I do,' Linda said. 'Some kind of inn perhaps.'

'They're not doing much business.'

'Not an inn then. A lodging-house.'

'Very few lodgers.'

'Don't worry about it, Steve. It doesn't matter.'

It was a woman who brought the next meal. She was plain and dumpy, probably Yuri's wife. Linda spoke to her and got the information that Yuri had gone out.

'I don't like that,' Brady said.

'You're too suspicious. He probably has work to do.'

'He may have gone to fetch the police.'

'There's no reason why he should.'

'It's time Wilkins was back,' Brady said.

The afternoon dragged away even more slowly than the morning. There was nothing to do but wait.

'Do you ever wonder whether you chose the right profession?' Brady asked. 'You could have made a stack of money as a model. Have you ever thought of that?'

'No, I haven't ever thought of that.'

'Are you making a lot of money at this game?'

'No.'

'Then why do it?'

'It's a job.'

'It's a hell of a job. And it's time Wilkins was back.'

But it was Yuri who came back first.

He brought the supper in. It was as late as that.

'Ask him where he's been,' Brady said.

'No; it's not our business.'

'It could be.'

'Why don't you forget it?' she said. 'If he had been to call the police they would have been here by now.' She was probably right about that. So maybe Yuri was trustworthy after all. Or maybe he simply knew nothing. But it was certainly time Wilkins came back. If he ever was coming back.

★ ★ ★

It was nearly midnight when they heard what sounded like a heavy lorry pulling into the yard. They were both awake, still waiting for Wilkins to return; Brady no longer with any real expectation that he would. In his own mind he had already written Wilkins off, and the question that plagued him was what to do now. With the Volvo stowed away in the garage of the Yalta Hotel in Moscow, they had no means of transport, and it was a long walk to the Finnish border. So what were the chances of thumbing a lift on the motorway? Pretty thin, to say the least. And even if they got to the border, what hope had they of slipping across when every frontier guard had probably been put on the alert to stop them?

The sound of the lorry set his nerves jangling. He got up from the settle on which he had been reclining and went to the window. He drew back the rough curtain and could just make out the massive shape of the vehicle. It looked like a big articulated van.

'Now what?'

'Come away from the window,' Linda said. 'Do you want to make yourself conspicuous?'

He let the curtain fall back into place. 'It's one of those big covered-in juggernauts,' he said. 'What's it doing here?'

'Perhaps this is a rest house for drivers.'

'So what are they going to think about us?'

She did not answer. Brady could see that she was worried. Wilkins ought to have been back, but Wilkins was never coming back now; that was certain.

He heard the doors of the cab slam, and a few seconds later there was the sound of heavy feet in the passageway outside the room. Then the door crashed open as though a gale of wind had struck it and a man came in. He was as big as Jaakko Karsten and had something of the look of Karsten about him. He was wearing a peaked leather cap and a leather jacket, and there was another man behind him who might have been his twin brother. Yuri was there too, hovering in the background.

'Are you ready?' the first man said in English.

Brady stared at him. 'Ready?'

The man laughed, and his laughter seemed to shake the room. 'Ah, of course, you do not know me. I am Johannes and this is Heikki.' He indicated with a flip of his broad hand the man behind him, and Brady noticed that he gave no surnames. 'We are

Finnish. We are to take you to Finland. Okay?'

'Okay,' Brady said.

It seemed about the only thing there was to say.

14

Long Way To Go

The packing-case was big enough for them to stand up inside it, and long enough and wide enough to allow them room to lie down if they wished. There was a mattress and there were a couple of pillows as furnishing. It was not luxurious, but as packing-cases went it might have been described as reasonably well appointed; there were a lot of packing-cases on the market that would have been far less comfortable.

Brady had felt a certain disquiet as Johannes and Heikki had screwed on the side; it was rather like being fitted into a coffin — an unusually large coffin, it was true, but one from which it would be impossible to escape without help from the outside. Fortunately, there was no risk of suffocating, since a number of holes had been drilled in the woodwork near the top and bottom, no doubt according to Wilkins's instructions, and there was plenty of fresh air getting in.

Brady had questioned Johannes about Wilkins, but the big Finn had been uninformative. He had just laid a finger along the side of his nose and had given Brady to understand that nothing was to be said on that subject. It was, however, apparent that they were to see no more of Wilkins for the present. Perhaps he had gone back to his duties with the party of young tourists, and Brady would not have been greatly surprised to learn that he had done just that; Wilkins was cool enough for anything. Yet it would have been taking an almighty risk after what had happened.

It was dark in the packing-case. Linda had a small torch in her handbag, but the battery would not have lasted long if they had left it switched on. So they travelled for the most part in darkness as the big vehicle thundered on its way towards Leningrad. Brady dozed in brief spells, waking suddenly to the realisation of the situation, glancing at his luminous watch, wondering how many kilometres they had covered, wondering about Wilkins, about the dead KGB men, about Vladimir, about Koulis.

'Do you think we'll get past the border post?'

He had sensed that the girl was awake as she lay beside him on the mattress, and she answered at once: 'I hope so, Steve, I hope so.'

'I hope so too,' he said. 'But I'm not counting on it. They may insist on opening this crate.'

'Why should they? There are plenty of other crates and this is probably a regular run. Do you think they open every crate every time?'

'They may have been warned about us and be extra vigilant.'

'It will be all right. Don't worry, Steve, don't worry.'

Her voice was very near to him, a whisper in his ear; he felt her lips brushing his cheek, and he put his arm round her waist and pulled her closer. If anyone could make him stop worrying, she was the one.

He was dozing off again when the van drew to a halt and he heard the engine die. It was suddenly very quiet and still inside the packing-case.

'We've stopped.'

'I know,' Linda said.

'Why?'

'I don't know.'

'It could be a road-block. They could be checking all vehicles.'

'You don't have to jump to conclusions,' she said.

He heard the back of the van being opened, the door rattling. Then he heard what sounded like somebody climbing into the van and some of the packing-cases being shifted, and he felt certain they had run into a police checkpoint and that a search was going on. He just hoped the police would not find the packing-case with the holes in it. But he knew they would.

He felt the girl's hand on his arm, squeezing it. They were both silent, not so much as whispering now for fear that even a whisper might be heard by the searchers, might reveal their presence. But mere silence was no sure defence against discovery. Brady heard the scrape of feet outside the packing-case and then the sound of the screws being removed. Then the wooden side was pulled away and daylight poured into the interior. He blinked up at the two men standing there.

'You want to go into the trees?' Johannes asked.

Brady did want to go into the trees, pretty urgently, but he was trying to see beyond the two Finns, looking for the uniforms of Russian police. Johannes must have read his thoughts, for he hastened to reassure him.

'Is okay. Nobody here but us. Be quick now. Then we eat. Then we go on.'

'You see,' Linda said. 'I told you not to jump to conclusions.'

She crawled out of the packing-case and made her way past the other crates to the tail of the van. Brady followed.

The vehicle had been pulled on to the

side of the road, and the trees to which Johannes had referred were part of an extensive forest. It was a grey morning, cloudy, with a moist feeling in the air. When Brady walked into the forest he could feel drops of water falling from the birch leaves like intermittent rain. When he returned to the van he found that the Finns had produced hot coffee and thick meat sandwiches. A few moments later the girl rejoined them.

Some lorries rumbled past and a car or two. Brady and the girl stayed inside the van, concealed from view, and as soon as they had finished eating they got back into the packing-case and Johannes and Heikki screwed the side on again. Brady heard the engine start up and felt the vibration as the huge vehicle got once more under way. After that it was the treatment as before — monotonous, rumbling on and on, with plenty of time to think and plenty of unpleasant things to think about.

'It was nicer in the Volvo.'

'You'd better forget the Volvo,' Linda told him.

'Do you think the hire firm will make me pay for it?'

'If I were you, I'd let Jaakko worry about that.'

'You think it was really his?'

'I shouldn't wonder.'

'Maybe he'll make me pay for it.'

'How much money have you got?'

'A handful of roubles and the promise of two hundred pounds.'

'Volvos cost more than that.'

'That's true. So maybe I had better let Jaakko do the worrying.'

'I don't think he's the worrying type.'

'Lucky Jaakko,' Brady said. 'Lucky, lucky Jaakko.' He knew somebody who was the worrying type, somebody who was going to worry like hell all the way to the frontier. He looked at his watch: the time was twenty minutes past nine. They had a long way to go.

★ ★ ★

In the afternoon they had another break for refreshment and a visit to the trees. It was just a small wood this time; beyond

251

the wood was a vast expanse of farmland, of ripening corn.

'Where are we now?' Brady asked.

'Ninety kilometres from Leningrad,' Johannes said.

'Shall we reach the border tonight?'

Johannes shook his head. 'We have to sleep.'

Brady had to admit that Johannes had a point there; he and Heikki had done a long stint and must be feeling tired.

'Where do you sleep?'

'Other side of Leningrad. In the cab.'

It would have pleased Brady better if they had planned to go straight on, but he did not argue; it would probably have been useless to do so anyway: the big Finns looked like men who would do it their own way, no matter what. He just hoped they ran into no trouble getting past Leningrad, but when he mentioned this to Johannes it produced a burst of laughter.

'Every week we come this way and never any trouble. Why we have trouble now?'

'No reason,' Brady said. 'But I just hope this isn't the time when you do.'

They seemed to be amused by the suggestion. Brady wished he could have found it as amusing as they did, but something seemed to have gone wrong with his sense of humour. Maybe it would put itself right when they were out of Russia.

Once again he and Linda were shut in the packing-case and the journey restarted. He dozed fitfully, woke to a sense of dismay, looked at his watch and tried to guess where they were, felt sick, had bouts of mild claustrophobia, and thought with deep nostalgic longing of a wretched little pad near Holloway Gaol which had never previously inspired him with anything but a feeling of mild disgust.

'Cobb,' he muttered. 'Stewart Cobb.'

'What about Stewart Cobb?' Linda asked.

'He said he could easily find someone else to do the job. I should have let him.'

'Oh, Steve,' she said, 'why do you have

to keep harping on it?'

'I should think I've got a right to harp.'

'You're lucky really. It could have been a lot worse.'

Brady tried to think how it could have been a lot worse, but it seemed a pretty fruitless exercise and he soon abandoned it.

He was dozing again when the stopping of the van woke him. The engine died and then he heard the rattle of the door and the sound of the crates being moved; and then again the side was unscrewed from the packing-case and the two Finns were standing there.

'We eat now,' Johannes said. 'Then we sleep. Okay?'

'But I thought you were going to sleep after getting past Leningrad.'

'So?' Johannes made a gesture with his arm towards the rear of the van. 'Leningrad is back there. You do not know we have passed it?'

'No,' Brady said. 'You get a poor view from inside a crate.'

Johannes and Heikki laughed; he had

made a joke. It was all one big joke to them.

'Have you noticed any unusual police activity along the road?' Linda asked. 'Anything at all out of the ordinary?'

Johannes shook his head. 'Nothing. All is normal.'

Brady hoped it would stay normal, but the real test had yet to come. He could not forget that they were still in Russia even though the scenery which met his eyes when he stepped down from the van was that of Karelia. The Finns had fought a war for this bit of country and had lost, because in the end it is never valour that wins wars but the power of the big battalions. And after that they had had to pay compensation to the victors. Which had been a bit hard on the Finns.

It was late in the evening but still light, and there was not going to be much darkness now that they were so far north again. There were plenty of trees around, and he did what he had to do and returned to the van. They ate a meal and got back into the packing-case, and he was feeling pretty sick of it by this time, but it was safer in there than it would have been hanging around outside.

It was very quiet after Johannes and Heikki had retired to the cab — just the occasional rumble of a heavy lorry going past on the highway and now and then the lesser sound of a car. Brady found sleep impossible to come by; he lay awake, fighting his claustrophobia and waiting for the hours to pass. They passed very slowly; more than once he suspected that his watch must have stopped, but when he put it to his ear he could hear it ticking away as regularly as ever.

'Why don't you go to sleep, Steve?' Linda said.

'How did you know I wasn't asleep?'

'You keep shifting about and sighing.'

'I don't believe it,' he said. 'Not sighing.'

'That's what it sounds like.'

'Well, maybe I've reason to sigh.'

'Maybe you have. Maybe we both have.'

'I keep thinking,' Brady said.

'What do you keep thinking?'

'I keep thinking it's an odd situation, being shut up in a wooden box with a beautiful girl somewhere on the road between Leningrad and Vyborg. Don't you think it's an odd situation? Or does it happen to you all the time?'

'Would you rather be shut up in a wooden box without the beautiful girl?'

'I'd rather it was between London and Reading,' Brady said. 'I'd be happier.'

'Perhaps we can arrange it some time,' she said.

He was still awake when Johannes and Heikki let them out for breakfast. He had not shaved for two days and was feeling as filthy as a piece of dried fish in a Cairo market. The Finns looked cheerful even at that hour, which was pretty early for looking cheerful.

'You have a good night?' Heikki asked; and he gave a grin which told Brady what he had in mind.

Brady did not bother to answer. He not only felt filthy, he also felt resentful of anyone who could be as cheerful as the Finns undoubtedly were. It made

257

him wonder what in hell they had to be cheerful about, driving a damned great articulated van back and forth between Helsinki and Moscow. Maybe they just liked to get away from their wives.

It was not raining but there was some cloud about and the air had the damp chill in it which it often had at that hour. They spent little time over breakfast and Brady had a poor appetite; the butterflies were busy again in his stomach. He noticed that Linda was not eating much either, so maybe she had some butterflies too. The Finns obviously had none.

'Okay then,' Johannes said. 'Now for the last lap.'

They got in. It seemed to Brady that the packing-case had acquired a certain odour; it had been too much lived in. He heard the screws being driven in, the back of the van being closed, the slam of the cab doors, the engine starting. The van began to move.

'Well,' he said, 'we shall soon know now.'

'It will be all right,' the girl said. She

was forever giving him little snippets of reassurance like that, trying to boost his morale. And it could do with some boosting. Or was she really trying to reassure herself? How could she be certain it would be all right? How could anyone?

'I wonder what's happened to Wilkins.'

'Don't worry about him. He'll be all right.'

She was at it again. He decided not to wonder what had happened to Vladimir; he doubted whether even she could have maintained that he would be all right.

★ ★ ★

He had not expected to fall asleep even though he had been awake all night, but he must have done so, for he awoke suddenly to the realisation that the van had stopped. He heard the slam of the cab doors and the sound of voices, and he knew that they must have reached the frontier. This was it; this was the pay-off; now they were going to discover whether Linda's often repeated assurances that they would be all right were just empty phrases or not.

He did not move, he did not say a word; he lay motionless and silent on the mattress, waiting. The girl was not moving and not saying anything either. They could have spoken softly and their words would not have been heard outside the van, but it was as though they were both preparing themselves for the moment when the door at the rear would be opened and the examination of the load would begin. When that happened the slightest movement, the slightest sound might give them away.

The rattle of the door sent a kind of answering vibration through Brady's nerves; he felt himself shivering, and he strove to control the shivering for fear it might communicate itself to the packing-case and even to the entire vehicle like a minor earth tremor, revealing without the faintest possibility of doubt that someone must be hiding there. His heart was pounding too, so that what with the shivering and the thumping it must surely seem to those outside that some kind of engine was at work inside the packing-case. The searchers simply could not miss it; he was certain that they could not.

And then he knew that he was right, that all his fears were only too well-founded, for they had not missed it. He heard the screws being withdrawn and felt an almost irresistible impulse to cry out, to get the moment of discovery finished with, to end the unendurable suspense once and for all.

But he remained silent, remained motionless; and then the side of the packing-case moved away and the daylight dazzled him briefly. He was aware of the girl getting to her feet and he stood up too, blinking at the light and trying to bring some moisture into his dry mouth. He could see Johannes and Heikki but no one else; and that was puzzling. He could not understand it; there should have been others, men in uniform, but there were not.

'Come,' Heikki said; and he put his hand on the girl's arm, guiding her to the back of the van.

Brady followed, making his way between

the crates, and when he reached the tail he could see no sign of any border post, no buildings of any kind; just Jaakko Karsten's Citroen parked at the side of the road and Jaakko himself standing beside it.

He got down from the van, and it still made no sense. 'Are we in Russia or Finland?'

'Finland,' Karsten said. 'Welcome back.'

Brady passed a hand across his eyes. He did not believe it. It was a trick, an illusion of some kind.

'What happened to the border? Did we fly over it?'

'You were asleep,' Linda told him. 'You slept through it all. I saw no point in waking you. You would only have been worried.'

He felt as though a great load had been lifted from his shoulders; he had an impulse to dance with joy but resisted it. 'Linda, you're a darling. Some day I'll do as much for you.'

'From here,' Jaakko Karsten said, 'you travel by car. It will be more comfortable, I think.'

Brady was still puzzled. 'You? How did you know?'

Karsten laughed. 'We have the telephone in Finland. Johannes called me from the Finnish side of the border. We arranged to meet here. It is simple really.'

Brady gathered that Karsten and the two truck drivers were not unacquainted.

'Let's go now,' Karsten said. 'No sense in hanging about here.'

Brady walked up to Johannes and shook him by the hand. 'Thank you for everything.'

Johannes grinned and shrugged. 'Is nothing. Any time.'

'There won't be any other time; you can take my word for that. Once is enough.'

He shook hands with Heikki too, thanked him too. Heikki just grinned.

Linda kissed them both. They seemed to like that.

15

Sea Dog

'We will go to the island,' Karsten said. 'You can stay there while we think of something. I have brought some clothes, so you can change and clean up.'

'You think of everything, Jaakko,' Linda said.

Karsten shook his head a little regretfully, it seemed. 'No, not everything.'

Brady guessed that he was referring to the events in Russia. They had told him briefly what had occurred and it was obvious that he was not happy about it; he frowned quite a lot during the recital, and he was not a man who was normally much given to frowning.

'And you still have the battery?'

'In my handbag,' Linda said.

'What will you do with it?'

'As soon as we get to the island I'm going to see what it really is.'

'You think you should do that?'

'Jaakko,' she said, and her voice was very cool, 'there's been some double-dealing somewhere along the line and I want to know where. It may help to solve the problem if we look at what's in that battery. I don't say it will, but it may. And besides, I'm curious.'

'Well, it's up to you.'

'Yes,' she said, 'it is up to me.'

It was clear that she was not prepared to listen to any argument on that point, and Karsten did not attempt any. Brady would have said that he was as keen as anyone to discover what the battery really was.

They reached the lake in less than an hour, driving fast over the rough roads and not talking a great deal, each perhaps thinking about the next move in the game. If it was a game. Brady had long since given up thinking of it in those terms; it was no game when men got killed for dubious stakes, no game at all.

Karsten parked the Citroen by the boathouse and got the speed-boat out.

They put the suitcases containing the clothes that Karsten had brought into the boat and got in too, and Brady was thinking of Koulis who would never again be borrowing this boat without permission; Koulis maybe waiting right now on the bank of the Styx for another kind of boat and old man Charon to ferry him across. Except that that was just a myth and the truth of it was that there was nothing left of Koulis but a body at the bottom of a lake in Russia. If it had not already been dredged up.

They reached the jetty, and Karsten made the boat fast and they walked up to the bungalow and climbed the steps to the veranda and went in. It was just as it had been when they left it; which was natural, since there had been nothing to alter it in the four days they had been away. Yet it seemed longer, and Brady felt that everything should have been changed, because it was not just four days that had passed; it was men's lives and trust and peace of mind and a hundred other things; small things perhaps and not easy to enumerate, but adding up to something big, something terribly, monstrously big. And yet the bungalow had not changed.

Karsten led the way into the room with the wide fireplace and the rug that Brady remembered from that other time when it really had begun to be like a genuine honeymoon; and he wished it could have stopped there. But it had had to go on, and it had got nastier all the way, and it was not finished yet.

Karsten said: 'You like a drink maybe?'

He did not wait for an answer but went off to get the drinks, and when he came back Linda already had the battery out of her handbag.

Karsten put the tray down on a small table. 'What you have?' He had brought whisky, brandy and vodka.

'I don't want a drink,' Linda said. 'I want a knife to slit this thing open.'

Karsten shrugged, took a penknife from his pocket and opened the blade He handed it to the girl.

'If the offer still holds,' Brady said, 'I could drink some whisky.'

Karsten poured the drink. 'Anything in it?'

'Straight,' Brady said.

Karsten gave him the glass and poured a vodka for himself. They both watched the girl getting to work on the battery.

She made a neat job of it. When she had peeled away the cardboard it could be seen that the terminals were dummies, not connected to anything because there were no electrical cells, just a rectangular tin box which might have contained sweets or cigarettes. But none of them believed that it did contain anything quite so commonplace.

There was a lid to the box, fastened with a strip of sticky tape. Linda Manning peeled off the tape and removed the lid. There was some packing. She removed that too.

'Ah!' she said. It was hardly louder than a sigh.

It was a piece of electronic equipment, several pieces in fact, miniaturised. It would have taken an expert in such things to have said just what the pieces added up to.

268

'So,' she said, 'this is what I was ordered to deliver to Vladimir.'

'But why?' Brady asked. 'What could he have done with that?'

He could see that she had already asked herself the same question and had come up with an answer.

'Nothing. It was never meant for him. Do you think it was meant for him, Jaakko?'

Karsten drank some vodka and said nothing.

'It was a set-up,' Linda said. 'I was to take it to Vladimir, but the KGB were to take it from there. As they nearly did. As they would most certainly have done if Wilkins had not stepped in.'

'You mean they knew about it?'

She nodded. 'That's exactly what I do mean. They knew all about it from the start. What do you think, Jaakko?'

Again she looked at Karsten. This time Karsten answered, 'I think you're right,' he said.

'But who — ?' Brady said.

Her gaze switched to him. He could see the passion in her eyes, the anger.

'Who gave it to me in London with precise instructions as to the way I was to take it into Russia and to whom I was to deliver it and where? Who set the whole thing up?'

Brady stared back at her. It hardly seemed possible. 'You mean Cobb?'

'Stewart Cobb,' she said. 'The bastard!'

'But why? Why would he do that?'

'For money. What else? I don't see him in the role of the innocent idealist.'

'But — '

'Oh, don't you see, Steve?' she said in sudden exasperation. 'Don't you see now? This is obviously some piece of secret military apparatus he's managed to get his hands on. He must have made a deal with the Russians, and maybe it's not the first time. Wilkins said somebody was dealing from the bottom of the pack, but even then I didn't begin to suspect Stewart; it just didn't enter my head that he might be the one.'

'Are you quite sure now?'

'It has to be him. Who else could it be? Who else even had their hands on the battery?'

'I did,' Karsten said.

She looked at him. 'Why, yes, you did, Jaakko. You put it in the radio. But you're not telling me you stripped it down and put the electronics in it?'

'No,' Karsten said, 'I'm not telling you that.'

'I trust you, Jaakko,' she said.

He drank the rest of his vodka and set the empty glass down on the tray. 'What will you do now?'

She thought about it. 'I must return to London. I'll confront him with the evidence. I'll get the truth out of him.'

'I've a better idea,' Karsten said.

She gave him a questioning glance.

'Get him to come out here.'

She thought about that too, and Brady could see that it appealed to her. The meeting would be less formal, and perhaps there was still some trifle of doubt in her mind as to whether she was right in suspecting Cobb.

'But will he come?'

'I think he will,' Karsten said, 'if you ask him.'

'Will you take me to a telephone?'

271

she said. There was not one in the bungalow.

'I think it would be better if you let me send a telegram for you. That way there can be no argument. He's bound to come.'

Brady saw that Karsten was no fool; but he had known that already.

'Very well,' Linda said. 'I'll write the message.'

* * *

Brady got the sauna going after Karsten had left. It had been arranged that Karsten should wait for Cobb to contact him on arrival in Helsinki and then go and pick him up. Always supposing Cobb took the bait. But none of them doubted that he would.

Brady had had a shave with a razor that was in the bungalow and felt less like a piece of human garbage. He lay on the shelf and let the steam of the sauna gradually ease the aches and pains out of his body, and he had been lying there no more than a few minutes when

Linda came in wearing the towelling bath-robe that was still much too big for her. As on the previous occasion that he remembered so well, she went into the dressing-room with scarcely a glance at him and came back without the robe. It was fairly steamy now, but he could see her clearly enough and she looked as good as she had looked the other time; and that was really saying something.

She came up to the shelf, and it was a wide shelf, and she said: 'Move over, Steve.' And then she lay down beside him and gave a long sigh, and he guessed she was letting all the tensions flow out of her, because there was nothing they had to do, nothing they had to worry about, until Cobb arrived.

'I'm glad we're out of Russia,' Brady said.

'I'm glad too,' she said.

'It's not that I've got anything against old Mother Russia; it's just that I don't feel comfortable there.'

'Do you feel comfortable here, Steve?'

'Comfortable and warm,' he said. And then: 'Do you think Cobb will bring me my two hundred quid?'

'I doubt it,' she said.

He sighed. 'That's the way I figured it. You know what I am, don't you?'

'What are you, Steve?'

'A born loser.'

She moved slightly closer to him, which was difficult because she had been very close before. 'I wouldn't say that, Steve darling. Not altogether. Would you?'

'No,' he said, thinking it over, 'maybe not. Not altogether.'

'And anyway,' she added after a while, 'I think you'll get your two hundred pounds even if Stewart doesn't bring it.'

'That will be nice,' Brady said. 'That will be very nice.'

★ ★ ★

They got up late the next day and lazed around. It was one of those bright warm northern days with the scent of the forests drifting across and flies hovering over the lake water. Brady felt too indolent even to push the small boat out and go fishing; he had never been keen on

274

fishing anyway, believing that fish had the right to be left unmolested. And that went for human beings too in his book. The trouble was that some human beings were never content to let other human beings get on with living in the way that suited them; they had to interfere. And that was what caused all the trouble in the world. Brady's Diagnosis.

'Do you think Cobb will be armed?' he said.

'I don't think so. What good would it do him?'

'But if he is?'

'Even if he is we've got nothing to worry about. There'll be three of us. What can he do?'

Brady saw the strength of her argument. Even if Cobb brought a gun, what could he do? Except maybe shoot himself.

Nevertheless, he paid a visit to the storeroom to make sure that the shotgun was still there and found that it was gone. It seemed strange, and he told Linda about it. She appeared unperturbed.

'What do you want with a shotgun?'

'I didn't say I wanted anything with it,

but why would Jaakko take it away?'

'Perhaps he thought it advisable after you shot the back door lintel full of holes. Perhaps he doesn't like people playing around with his guns. Were you thinking of shooting Stewart?'

'I thought it might be a wise precaution to keep it handy.'

'There's no need,' she said. 'Nobody's going to do any shooting.'

'I hope not,' Brady said. 'There was enough of that in Moscow. Guns scare me.'

'So why did you want the shotgun?'

'Not my guns. Other people's.'

'Nobody's going to scare you this time,' she said.

He hoped she was right, but he would have felt safer with the shotgun lying around where he could get his hands on to it.

* * *

It was well on into the evening when they heard the sound of the speed-boat. They went out to the veranda and could see it coming, slicing the water like a plough and leaving a wedge of foam behind it.

. 'Do we go to meet them?' Brady said.

Linda shook her head. 'Let's wait for them here. It's going to be embarrassing enough anyway.'

Brady saw what she meant. Cobb was her immediate superior and it was not going to be the easiest thing in the world to accuse him of being a double-agent, a traitor to his country. Yet the promptness with which he had come out to Finland in answer to her message surely supported the theory of his guilt: an innocent man might have wanted rather more information before leaving London.

They watched Karsten make the boat fast to the jetty, and then the two men started walking up the path to the bungalow. Cobb was wearing a grey summer suit and carrying a small suitcase, which seemed to indicate that he expected to be staying the night. He looked as sleek as ever, and if he was suffering any qualms of conscience or misgivings regarding the imminent interview with the agent he had sent to Russia on such a disastrous mission, he was certainly concealing the fact very well. Indeed, he could not have appeared less perturbed if he had merely arrived on the island for the purpose of spending a quiet week-end away from it all. He mounted the veranda steps ahead of Karsten, and Brady noticed that he avoided touching the handrail with his fingers, as though fearful of picking up some contamination from the weathered timber. He had not altered.

'Ah, my dear Linda,' he said when he reached the top. 'How nice to see you again. And looking so well too. Obviously your spell away from London has not done you any harm.'

The girl pressed her lips together but said nothing, and Cobb's gaze shifted to Brady. 'And you, Stephen, you look pretty healthy too. Rude health, eh?' He smiled, but his eyes were giving that impression of polished steel which Brady remembered from their first meeting. He remembered too that Cobb had never before called him Stephen, and he was not at all sure he liked the way Cobb spoke the name now — as if with a hint of mockery.

'It could have been a lot less rude,' he said. 'It could have been very sickly. A couple of days ago I wouldn't have given much for its chances.'

'Ah,' Cobb said. 'Yes, I believe things did become a trifle rugged.'

'That's putting it mildly.'

'I warned you there might be some slight danger when you took the job.'

'I'm not sure I would have called it slight.'

'Well, that of course is a matter of opinion. But why are we all standing out here? Why don't we go inside and talk things over like civilised people?'

He began moving towards the door. Already he seemed to have taken charge, and that was not the way it should have been. Brady was not quite sure what he had expected of Cobb — a bit of grovelling perhaps; if so, he was being disappointed; Cobb was certainly not grovelling; he seemed absolutely sure of himself, completely in control of the situation. It was certainly not as it should have been.

He walked into the bungalow and the others followed him. He put the small suitcase down and led the way to the room with the big fireplace. Brady wondered whether he had been there before or whether he was simply going by instinct.

As if by mutual agreement but without a word, they all sat down round the wide hearth.

'Now,' Cobb said, looking at Linda Manning, 'suppose you tell me all about it.'

Brady could see that, now that the moment had arrived, she was at a loss to know how to begin. After a few fruitless attempts she got up suddenly and went out of the room. Cobb examined his fingernails, which were in perfect condition; Brady and Karsten watched him examining them. No one said a word.

Linda came back carrying the tin with the electronic equipment in it. She set the tin down on the small table at the side of Cobb's chair.

'Perhaps,' she said, 'you will tell me what that is.'

Cobb glanced at it cursorily, then up at her. 'You had no instructions to open it.'

'Never mind what instructions I had. I want to know what it is.'

'It's Sea Dog,' Cobb said.

She stared at him. 'Sea Dog?'

'Ah,' he said, 'of course that means nothing to you. Sea Dog is the code name for a new naval missile still on the secret list. Highly important in the NATO scheme of things incidentally. This — ' he gave a little flutter of the hand in the direction of the tin — 'is the heart of the weapon — something to do with the guidance system, so I believe. I am also given to understand that it is a most sophisticated device, though of course I lack the technical knowledge to follow the precise working of the thing.'

'And you were selling it to the Russians?'

'They are very interested in it. Naturally

enough, since it is a NATO weapon.'

'And you were selling it to them?' She still seemed scarcely able to believe it, although it was merely confirmation of her own deductions.

'I still hope to do so,' Cobb said coolly. 'New arrangements will have to be made now that you have failed me. But we shall manage; yes, we shall certainly manage.'

She stared at him in disbelief. 'You can't be serious.'

Cobb's expression was bland to the point of innocence. 'But why not, my dear, why not?'

'Because we know about it. That's why not.'

'Certainly that is unfortunate,' Cobb said. 'Unfortunate for me, but more especially for you.' He slipped a hand inside his jacket and when it reappeared it was holding a small automatic pistol. 'You know, don't you, what traditionally happens to people who know too much.'

She stepped back. Brady had seen her handle a gun like that, but he knew that she was not carrying one now, that she had not brought one to Finland. But Cobb had.

'Don't be a fool, Stewart,' she said. 'You can't — '

'Stop!' he said. 'Please don't disappoint me by saying I can't get away with it. Such a cliché. And simply not true, not even true. I can get away with it and I shall.'

'You propose to shoot the three of us?'

Brady glanced at Karsten and was relieved to see that he also had produced a pistol. It looked like one of those Colt forty-fives which over the course of many years must have been turned out by the thousand. He was a big man and he probably needed a big gun.

Cobb was not looking at him and even seemed to have forgotten his existence.

'That will not be necessary,' he said. 'Not the three of you.'

Brady did not get it at once; but then it hit him and again the ground was shifting under his feet.

'Jaakko is my man,' Cobb said. 'Didn't you know?'

16

In the Nick

Brady and Linda were sitting on one side of the hearth and Cobb on the other. Karsten had put his gun away and was pouring drinks. He offered one to the girl, but she refused with a certain contempt which seemed to touch him a little; Brady thought he flinched slightly. Brady himself accepted a whisky; he felt he needed it, and the way things were going it might well be the last he would ever have.

Cobb had laid his small pistol on the table beside his chair; it was there for him to reach in a moment if he should need it, but no one was trying to rush him.

'Why, Jaakko?' Linda said. 'Why?'

He did not answer.

'I can understand Stewart's motive,' she said. 'He did it for the money. But you didn't need money and I thought you hated the Russians.'

'I do,' Karsten muttered, and he seemed to be in pain, his face twisted. 'I do.'

'Then why?'

'Every man has his price,' Cobb said, and he gave a venomous little snigger which sounded almost obscene. 'Even Jaakko. He could have lost everything. The Russians were on to him, you see, and they could have brought pressure to bear on the Finnish authorities; you know how sensitive they are in such matters. Jaakko didn't dare risk that, did you, Jaakko? Especially with all those fat government contracts of yours. You had to co-operate.'

Brady could guess who had put the Russians on to Karsten. Cobb had certainly had it all figured out.

'So now you intend to shoot us,' Linda said. She glanced at Karsten. 'I shouldn't have listened to you, Jaakko. I should have gone back to London the way I intended. But you persuaded me that this was the better idea. And I thought you were my friend.'

Again Karsten flinched. He could not meet the accusation in her eyes.

'Don't blame him,' Cobb said, giving a cynical grin. 'With so much at stake, what was he to do? But as to shooting you, no, I think not. Far too crude. I fancy something more in the line of a boating accident. So terribly sad. Such an attractive young couple cut off in the prime of life. On their honeymoon too.'

'And you think that will cover you?'

He smiled at her tauntingly. 'Don't you?'

She shook her head. 'You've forgotten Wilkins. He's no fool; he'll put two and two together and come up with Stewart Cobb.'

'That meddling idiot,' Cobb said with a brief flash of anger. 'If it had not been for him none of this would have been necessary.'

'He mucked things up for you, didn't he?'

'Yes, he did,' Cobb said; and Brady saw that Karsten must have told him about Wilkins's part in the affair. Obviously Karsten would have given him the whole story. 'But we do not have to worry our heads about Charles Wilkins. Our friends across the border will deal very effectively with him, I think.'

'You really are a swine, aren't you?' Linda said. 'But you're still not quite out of the wood.'

Cobb gave her a sharp look. 'What exactly do you mean by that?'

'I mean that somebody must have alerted Wilkins. And that rather points to the fact that someone in London has suspicions regarding your activities. You'll need to be careful, Stewart, you'll need to be very careful, because one day you're going to be stabbed in the back.'

He retorted again with a spurt of anger: 'You can leave that to me. I can handle that.'

'Perhaps,' she said. 'But there still remains the matter of the late George Koulis, doesn't there?'

Cobb's head jerked up. She had touched him at last; she had introduced a name that was new to him.

'Koulis? Who is Koulis?'

'Was, Stewart, was. Past tense Didn't

Jaakko tell you about him? Koulis was an American who seemed to take a great interest in us. He turned up first in a blue Saab in Porvoo. Then he came out here one night with the intention of breaking into the place, but Steve frightened him off with Jaakko's shotgun. Finally he broke into the Volvo at a camping site on the road to Leningrad, and Steve had to kill him, I'm afraid. Bad thing, killing a CIA man.'

Cobb looked at Brady with narrowed eyes. 'Is this true?'

'It's true,' Brady said. 'And I wish to God it wasn't. My killing him was an accident.'

'What did you do with the body?'

'Dropped it in a lake.'

Cobb turned to Karsten accusingly. 'You didn't tell me the CIA were in on this.'

Karsten looked uneasy. 'We don't know he was a CIA man; that's only conjecture. He could have been nothing but a petty thief.'

'Oh, of course.' Cobb was heavily sarcastic. 'Petty thieves are given to following people for hundreds of miles, across frontiers, up hill and down dale; it's the usual thing. And what, might one ask, was this petty thief trying to steal?'

'The battery, of course,' Linda said. 'What else?'

'So who put him on to it? Who gave him the tip-off?'

Brady glanced at Karsten, and there was a guilty look on Karsten's face. And suddenly it hit Brady. Koulis had indeed been a CIA man and Karsten knew it. Karsten knew it because it was he who had tipped Koulis off. Jaakko doing the double-double-cross as a sop to his conscience, as a way of foiling Cobb and the Russians without appearing to do so. Only it had not worked out; Koulis had died and Jaakko had failed there too. Brady had once called him lucky Jaakko, but perhaps he was not so lucky after all.

It seemed not to have occurred to Cobb, and he thought about giving Cobb the hint in the hope of causing a split between him and Karsten. But then he decided not to, not yet, because there might be a better way: if Karsten really had tipped Koulis off, then it showed that he was not whole-heartedly with Cobb, and if they could only get him by himself they might play on his better instincts and even yet bring him round to their side. It was a slim chance certainly, but it was worth a try.

And then Linda said: 'It was probably someone in London. Another one to watch, Stewart darling.' She was rubbing in the salt, and it occurred to Brady that maybe she too had guessed that Karsten was the man and was trying to head Cobb off from that line of thought.

If so, she was succeeding, for he gave her a savage look and said: 'I can deal with them: don't think I can't. But you, my dear Linda, won't be around to see me do it.'

'So you still intend to remove us?'

'You've said nothing to make me change my mind.'

'Well,' she said, 'I won't argue with you and I won't plead with you either, because I'm quite sure that wouldn't be any use.'

'It wouldn't.'

'But there is just one question I'd like to ask — simply out of curiosity. What should I really have been taking to Vladimir?'

Brady glanced at Karsten and saw that the guilty look had gone now that the discussion had shifted away from the subject of George Koulis. It confirmed his suspicion that Karsten was the one who had alerted Koulis.

Cobb also seemed to have regained his composure. 'Well,' he said, 'there seems to be no good reason for not telling you now. Funnily enough, it was another kind of electronic device — a miniaturised radio transmitter in fact.'

'Yet Vladimir knew nothing about it.'

Cobb smiled complacently, apparently enjoying himself again, now that he was once more displaying his own cleverness. 'Well, no. I was supposed to have arranged that, you see. But why bother, since he was never going to get the thing anyway? No point in raising the poor fellow's hopes.'

'How considerate of you.'

'Wasn't it?'

Cobb turned to Karsten. 'Is there somewhere safe where we can put your guests for a time?'

'There's the sauna,' Karsten said. 'We can padlock the door.'

Cobb reached for his pistol and stood up. 'Come along then.'

Neither Brady nor Linda made any move. Cobb gestured impatiently with the gun. 'Now don't be obstinate. You know we can use force if necessary.'

Brady shrugged and stood up. What Cobb said was true; it would be futile to resist. And perhaps it would be possible to break out of the sauna. Linda also stood up.

'That's better,' Cobb said. 'A bit of co-operation always helps. Now let's be moving.'

Karsten led the way, Brady and Linda followed, while Cobb, watchful and with the gun in his hand, brought up the rear. Karsten opened the door of the sauna house and stood aside to let them walk in. With the stove unlighted, it was cool inside. The door closed behind them and they heard the sound of the padlock being fastened and then the footsteps of the two men as they walked away.

'And now,' Linda said, 'I suppose we try to find a way out.'

'It is the obvious thing to do,' Brady agreed.

But a close inspection soon convinced him that Karsten had known what he was about when he had suggested the sauna as a prison. The walls were of stout timber and so was the door. Admittedly there were two windows, but they were small and near the roof. The framework looked strong, and even if they could have broken it the noise would almost certainly have been audible in the bungalow, bringing Cobb and Karsten very quickly on the scene.

'I don't think we're going to break out.'

'So you're going to sit down and wait for them to come for us?' Linda said.

'Do you think Cobb will really do what he threatened?'

'He'll do it. He's ruthless and he's got to protect himself. If he lets us live he's finished and he knows it. Oh, he'll do it even if it has to be by shooting.'

Brady had to agree that she was probably right. Cobb certainly gave an impression of cold ruthlessness, and certainly he had not flown out to Finland to reason with them. But there remained Karsten.

'I think Jaakko tipped off Koulis.'

'That's what I think,' Linda said. 'But it didn't work out the way he wanted it to, did it?'

'No, but it means that Jaakko isn't a hundred per cent with Cobb.'

'He wants to save his own skin though, and to do that he has to row in with him.'

'All the same, if we could work on Jaakko we might bring him round to our side.'

'It's unlikely, but we could certainly try if we had him here. But we haven't.'

'That's true,' Brady said. 'So I'd better get to work on one of those windows.'

There were some birch logs by the stove. He picked one up, but he could only just reach the window with his arm outstretched, and he was looking round for something to stand on when he heard the sound of footsteps outside. He dropped the log.

'Somebody's coming.'

It was Karsten. He unlocked the door and came in warily. He was not holding his gun but it was stuck in the waistband of his trousers where he could get his hand on it in a moment. He was carrying a tray on which were sandwiches and two cups of coffee.

'We're eating,' he said gruffly. 'You want some?'

'A last meal for the condemned prisoners?' Brady said. 'Nice thought, Jaakko.'

Karsten did not meet his eyes. He put the tray on one of the shelves and began to back towards the door.

'Wait,' Linda said.

He halted, uneasy, still not looking directly at them, but still wary, his right hand hovering over the butt of the big Colt.

'Why did you put Koulis on to us, Jaakko?'

He started, but he did not deny it. He just said nothing.

'It was because you didn't like what you were being forced to do, wasn't it? So you figured that if a CIA man picked up the battery it would be all right, because the CIA would know how to deal with Cobb. That's what you thought, isn't it?'

Still Karsten said nothing, but she kept at him.

'You can still make things all right, Jaakko. Let us go. Let us deal with Stewart. You don't have to do a thing except give us that gun and leave the door open.'

He dropped his hand on the butt of the Colt. 'No.'

'Why not, Jaakko? You're on our side really. You don't like helping the Russians. Be a man, Jaakko; do it the way you'd really like to do it.'

He was wavering; she had him going; Brady could see that. A little more pressure and he might do it. Brady did not say a word, did not move; if anyone could talk Karsten round to their side it was the girl.

'Give us the gun, Jaakko,' she said, and her voice was soft and persuasive; she might have been speaking words of love. 'Give it to me, Jaakko.'

He almost did it. He half pulled the Colt from his belt, but then some thought of what the consequences might be must have come into his head, stopping him in the act.

'No,' he said again; and he turned abruptly away and made a move towards the door.

But he had made the fatal mistake; he had turned his back on them. Brady stooped and reached for the birch log, and Karsten heard him and got the gun out and began to turn. But not fast enough, not nearly fast enough. Brady hit him just above the left ear and the gun went off as he fell.

Karsten lay on the floor of the sauna with a little blood coming from his head, and Brady dropped the log and picked up the Colt.

'He told me another time I'd better

hit him with a log. He told me.'

'And now?' the girl said.

'Now we go and get Cobb.'

But there was no need; Cobb was there; he had appeared in the doorway as silently as a shadow, and he had the small automatic in his hand.

'You had better drop the Colt,' he said; and the small automatic was pointing unwaveringly at Brady's stomach.

The Colt was hanging slackly in Brady's hand; before he had even begun to raise it Cobb could have put a bullet in him.

'Drop it,' Cobb said.

Brady dropped it. There was nothing else to do.

'That was wise,' Cobb said. He glanced down at Karsten. 'You shouldn't have hit Jaakko. He's got a temper and he'll be mad at you.'

'I know,' Brady said. 'I hit him once before. He said if I did it again he'd break my arm.'

He saw that Karsten was beginning to stir; he must have a hard head. Karsten gave a groan and sat up. He put a hand to the place where Brady had hit him and then looked at the blood on his fingers; then he looked at Brady.

'You hit me.'

'Yes,' Brady said.

Karsten was certainly mad at him; his head must have been hurting and he had been made to look a fool. He reached out and got a grip on the big Colt, and Brady thought for a moment that he was going to shoot. But he did not; he got to his feet, took one step to bring himself within range, swung the gun in a narrow arc.

Brady tried to get out of the way and was too late. The metal hit him on the side of the head, and he heard the girl give a cry as though she had felt the pain herself; and then nothing more, because that was when the lid closed on him, and Karsten and Cobb and Linda vanished from sight, and everything else vanished too, like a slate being washed clean.

* * *

They were down by the lake then. He was lying on the shingle where somebody — and it had to be Karsten — must have dumped him. Things were a bit hazy and the light was not as good as it had been, and he almost drifted off into unconsciousness again; but then he heard the girl scream, and that really brought him awake.

He sat up and saw Karsten knee-deep in the water. He was carrying the girl and she was struggling to break free, but he was too strong for her. Cobb was standing a few yards from the edge of the water, not getting his shoes wet, and he still had the small automatic in his hand. He was looking quietly on, and Brady did not immediately realise what Karsten was doing. And then the girl stopped screaming very abruptly because Karsten had stooped and thrust her under the water. And he was holding her there.

Brady knew then what was happening: this was part one of the boating accident — only it was no accident, and he would not have believed Karsten capable of doing it if he had not seen it happening. But Karsten was mad, he was really mad after that thump on the head, mad enough for anything.

Brady got to his feet, and his legs felt rubbery and his head was drumming. But he went at a staggering run, bent forward in a crouching posture, and his shoulder hit Cobb at the base of the rib cage, and Cobb gave a sobbing gasp and went down. Brady did not wait for him to get up; he kicked him in the mouth and went after Karsten. He hit Karsten on the throat and gave him the knee and everything else that was dirty and potentially lethal. And Karsten let the girl go and she came up spluttering.

Karsten started to fight back, but Brady took him from behind with an arm lock round the neck, and he put his knee in again and gave a jerk, and Karsten was down in the water with Brady holding him there to see how he liked it.

Karsten might have drowned then if Cobb had not interfered. Brady knew Cobb was back in business when the girl sang out in warning; and then he heard the crack of that little automatic, and something slammed into his right arm just above the elbow and he let

301

Karsten go because there was no more strength in that arm.

He faced Cobb, standing in the water with the arm hanging limp, and he saw Cobb taking careful aim and the blood running from his mouth and down his chin, running on to his clean white shirt and his tie. He did not move; he heard the girl cry out again, and he knew that Cobb was going to kill him and he could do nothing, nothing except wait for the bullet to bore a hole in his chest and in his heart.

He heard the cracking sound again, but felt nothing, and he could not understand how Cobb could have missed. At that range it should not have been possible. And then he saw Cobb's knees begin to bend and the gun drop from his hand, and a moment later he was stretched out on the shingle, jerking a little but not trying to get up, because he was never again going to get up under his own power.

Brady heard a foot crunch on the shingle, and he turned his head and saw Wilkins standing there with a gun in his hand; Wilkins grinning a shade savagely, it seemed, like a man who had been through a lot of nastiness but had at last paid off the score, had paid it off in full.

'Well, old man,' he said, 'it looks as if I got here in the nick, doesn't it? Right in the bloody nick, as the saying is.'

17

Jigsaw

Brady was working on a jigsaw puzzle when Linda Manning walked in. Doing a jigsaw puzzle was the kind of work that did not put too great a strain on his right arm, which was still convalescent.

'Don't you knock on doors these days?' he asked. 'Or is that a bit old hat?'

'I didn't want to put you to the trouble of getting up and opening it,' she said. 'I know you're still a sick man.'

'Ha!' he said; and he gave her a long, careful inspection and came to the conclusion that she looked very smart in a brown dress with yellow sleeves and an embroidered bolera to match.

She sounded pretty cheerful too, and he wondered how she managed to recover so quickly from a nasty sticky business like that honeymoon caper in Finland

and Russia. But he supposed that when it was the kind of business you did for a living you got used to it. No doubt it was meat and drink to people like Charles Wilkins.

Nevertheless, he doubted whether even Wilkins would ever be going back to Russia. He had got out by the skin of his teeth, it seemed, though precisely how he had not seen fit to tell them; merely saying that there were ways and means and that not everybody crossed the border at the official crossing-points. But he was not likely to put his head in that trap again. Besides, thanks to Cobb, the KGB were on to him, so his usefulness as an agent in that part of the world was finished anyway.

Nor would Cobb be doing any more in the double-agent line: he had ended up, like the late Mr. Koulis, being sunk in the middle of a lake; which seemed to be the best thing to do with him. Jaakko Karsten they had left to his own devices; there would have been no point in killing him, since it would merely have caused a deal of trouble. And, as even Wilkins had to admit, there had been enough killing already.

Brady had at first been puzzled as to how Wilkins had got on to the island without a boat, but it appeared that he had circled the lake and had stumbled upon an old punt hidden in the reeds and had ferried himself across in that.

'Bit of luck, old man. If I hadn't found it I'd have had to swim, and I'm not keen on swimming.'

Brady was glad Wilkins had not had to swim; it might have made him late.

* * *

Linda Manning looked at the jigsaw laid out on Brady's table. 'What's it going to be when it's finished?'

'Queen Elizabeth the Second.'

'It looks more like a ship to me.'

'It is a ship. Haven't you ever heard of the Q.E.2?'

'Oh that Queen Elizabeth,' she said. 'Would you like me to make some tea?'

'If you don't mind the squalid surroundings,' Brady said; and he remembered how Cobb had shuddered at the very idea of drinking tea in that room.

She laughed. 'I've got a strong constitution.'

He watched her filling the kettle and spooning tea into the old brown pot, and he thought it was nice having her there and not having to worry about men in blue Saabs or big black saloons. And he wondered what she had done with that phoney marriage certificate. Not that it mattered.

'By the way,' she said, 'I've been talking to some of our people and they think we might be able to use you.'

Brady shuddered all the way down his spine and through the soles of his feet. 'You have used me.'

'On a more permanent basis.'

'Holy saints above! You mean take a job with your lot?'

'Well, it's not definite. You'd have to be interviewed and vetted.'

'Vetted? What do they take me for? A horse?'

'Don't be silly. It's the normal routine.

And then you'd be sent on a course.'

He shuddered again. 'I don't think I could stand that.'

'You could if you tried.'

'What about my pusillanimity?'

'I think you make far too much of that. I don't think you're at all pusillanimous when it comes to the crunch.'

'It's coming to the crunch that I don't like.'

The kettle began to boil and she made the tea. 'Think about it, Steve.'

'All right,' he said, 'I'll think about it.' There was no harm in thinking.

She poured the tea and handed him a cup. He took a sip from it and set it down beside the jigsaw puzzle.

'There's one piece that doesn't fit in.'

'Oh?'

'That man at the tube station who tried to push you in front of a train.'

'You're thinking of another jigsaw,' she said.

'Who was he working for? It couldn't have been for Cobb or the Russians and it couldn't have been for the CIA. None of them would have gained anything by doing you in. Not then. So who was it?'

'Oh,' she said, 'I thought you'd heard about him. He'd escaped from a mental institution.'

'You mean it was just a coincidence? Nothing to do with our business at all?'

'Nothing.'

'I don't like that. It's untidy.'

'I'm sorry, Steve,' she said. 'but that's the way it is. In life you never get every piece to fit in. I think they use the wrong kind of saw.'

He drank some more tea. She was probably right. She had a way of being right.

She opened her handbag and he thought for a moment she was going to pull out that gun she sometimes carried in there; but it was not a gun, it was something far nicer to look at — a roll of banknotes. She put the roll on the table.

'Your two hundred pounds.'

'So they paid up?'

'Of course. They're very honest where money is concerned.'

'Honest enough to pay me compensation for the gear I lost in Moscow?'

'Now, Steve darling,' she said, 'you mustn't expect miracles. Would an evening on the town with a beautiful girl be compensation enough?'

'I'll settle for that,' Brady said.

THE END

MURDER AS USUAL
Hugh Pentecost

A psychotic girl shot and killed Mac Crenshaw, who had come to the New England town with the advance party for Senator Farraday. Private detective David Cotter agreed that the girl was probably just a pawn in a complex game — but who had sent her on the assignment?

THE MARGIN
Ian Stuart

It is rumoured that Walkers Brewery has been selling arms to the South African army, and Graham Lorimer is asked to investigate. He meets the beautiful Shelley van Rynveld, who is dedicated to ending apartheid. When a Walkers employee is killed in a hit-and-run accident, his wife tells Graham that he's been seeing Shelly van Rynveld . . .

TOO LATE FOR THE FUNERAL
Roger Ormerod
Carol Turner, seventeen, and a mystery, is very close to a murder, and she has in her possession a weapon that could prove a number of things. But it is Elsa Mallin who suffers most before the truth of Carol Turner releases her.

NIGHT OF THE FAIR
Jay Baker
The gun was the last of the things for which Harry Judd had fought and now it was in the hands of his worst enemy, aimed at the boy he had tried to help. This was the night in which the past had to be faced again and finally understood.

MR CRUMBLESTONE'S EDEN
Henry Crumblestone was a quiet little man who would never knowingly have harmed another, and it was a dreadful twist of irony that caused him to kill in defence of a dream . . .

PAY-OFF IN SWITZERLAND
Bill Knox

'Hot' British currency was being smuggled to Switzerland to be laundered, hidden in a safari-style convoy heading across Europe. Jonathan Gaunt, external auditor for the Queen's and Lord Treasurer's Remembrancer, went along with the safari, posing as a tourist, to get any lead he could. But sudden death trailed the convoy every kilometer to Lake Geneva.

SALVAGE JOB
Bill Knox

A storm has left the oil tanker S.S. *Craig Michael* stranded and almost blocking the only channel to the bay at Cabo Esco. Sent to investigate, marine insurance inspector Laird discovers that the Portuguese bay is hiding a powder keg of international proportions.